Twelve Nights

A dozen Christmas horrors

———

Written by Katherine Kitchener
Illustrated by Kelly Bastow

TWELVE NIGHTS
Copyright © 2022 by Katherine Kitchener

For information contact:
spookatherine@gmail.com

Cover and interior art by Kelly Bastow

ISBN 978-0-6487454-2-6

First edition December 2022

Table of Contents

KATHERINE KITCHENER

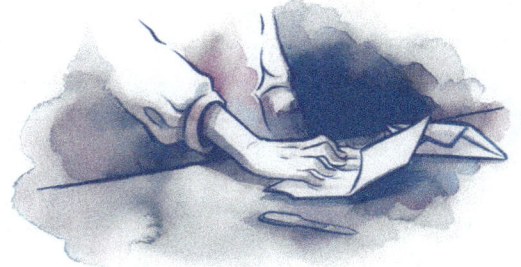

HAS IT REALLY BEEN A YEAR?

DEAREST FRIENDS,

Has it really been a year? How fast the time has gone. It feels like the years get shorter and shorter. I'm sorry that I haven't been as good at keeping in touch as I'd have liked to be. We've been terribly busy, but who hasn't? Hopefully this short message will serve to catch you all up on what our family has been up to this year.

This hasn't been the easiest year for us. I know we all face trials in life, but sometimes it feels like our family has been specifically singled out. Aaron has been spending more and more time at work and it feels like we hardly see him these days. Despite this, he was passed over for promotion (again). Still, he seems to get some satisfaction from being the best at what he does, even if we can never afford that holiday he promised.

Sarah has had her own struggles, too. Her schoolwork has started to decline ever since she started seeing the latest in what feels like an endless string of boyfriends. Really, there have been so many I have lost count. There's something different about this current one, though.

As for Dean, well he's finally home. Ever since he got back he has been moody and withdrawn, but that's teenage boys I suppose.

For my own part, I have taken up a new hobby – stonework. I know what you're thinking. It's such a different hobby for a woman. I suppose I have always been unique that way, wouldn't you say? I must say, there's something so rewarding about making something with your own hands. Most recently I made a birdbath, though no birds seem to have used it yet. There haven't been any birds around the garden for a while now. Ever since Dean returned from you-know-where, actually. The next project I'm working on is something really special. They'll be Christmas presents for Aaron and the kids... provided I can get them finished in time!

On those rare times when Aaron is home, things have been quieter than usual. Aaron used to be so hard on poor Dean, but now they don't argue at all. In fact, they barely speak to each other at all. When Dean looks at his father he no longer has that heartbreaking expression of a fearful child. In fact, it may seem funny to say, but sometimes it is almost as though Aaron is afraid of Dean.

TWELVE NIGHTS

A couple of months ago Sarah finally had her wisdom teeth out. They've been getting infected on a pretty regular basis, to the extent that she was suffering from fevers, so it's a relief to finally have those gone. Most of the teeth came out easily, but the fourth was all gnarled and crooked, with the root wrapped partly around Sarah's jawbone. The dentist almost broke her jaw ripping it out! I don't know what happened to the other three teeth, but Sarah keeps that last one in a glass of milk on her bedside table. She refills the milk every day, but it still smells sour. She seems to like the smell, though. I did joke to her that the tooth fairy would not be able to see the tooth hidden in that milk, but she didn't give much of a response. Teenagers can be so difficult to connect with. Sometimes I feel so out of touch with my own children.

I do have to admit, though, that Dean is helping out a lot more around the house ever since he got home. He takes it upon himself to take the rubbish out whenever the kitchen bin is full. He seems so much stronger now. A real young man. Strangely, when I take the wheelie bin out to the curb once a week it doesn't feel as heavy as I think it should. Perhaps I am getting stronger, too! Dean has taken up cooking, too. He is such an efficient cook. Whenever Dean prepares a meal there is never so much as a scrap of meat or fat or gristle left. When I gather the finished plates, Dean's bones are always picked clean – the marrow sucked right out.

Some of you will be pleased to hear that Aaron and I finally took your advice and started marriage counselling. I really think it's working, too! True, there are still times, too many times, when Aaron won't so much as look me in the eye, but I just can't wait to see his face when I give him his Christmas present.

Aaron has been drinking more than usual, which is a bit of a sticking point during our counselling sessions... but at least the kids know what to get him for Christmas! He used to drink Johnny Walker blue label, but does not seem to be so fussy these days. A little while ago I made a joke about an acetone-soaked rag being sufficient and earned myself a black eye. Still, what's a little love tap between soulmates?

Sarah spends a lot of time now reading. Really, the amount of time she spends with her nose stuck in some book or other, I really don't understand why her school marks are suffering. They tend to be big books, too. Old and musty and leather-bound. Sarah is oddly protective of them, but I don't know why because no one else in the family is a bookworm.

Dean is so moody sometimes that I wonder if I actually have two daughters! Every month or so he gets noticeably worse. He spends a long time in the bathroom (you should see what he does to the razors!). I hear him moving about the house at night and I think he is sneaking out, but Aaron just tells me to mind my own business.

It is with great sadness, however, that I have to inform you of the passing of my dear little Presto, who was mauled to death some weeks ago. He was such a lovely little dog. My best friend, really. No one else in the family really seems to care, though.

That's where I got the idea for the Christmas presents, actually. The way I see I, we show how much we love someone by the care and dignity we show them in death. So I'm personally crafting tombstones for the family. I'm virtually finished and I must say they're almost perfect. My best work yet. Something is not quite right about them, though. They just look so odd without a date. December 25th has a jolly ring to it.

Seasons greeting from our family to yours,
The Ericksons

SHOE FAIRY

VANESSA TAPPED HER FEET in time with the smooth beats coming through her headphones, except that in her cherry-red Doc Martins it was less of a *tap, tap, tap* and more of a *clomp, clomp, clomp*. She wasn't actually listening to the music, not carefully anyway. It was more of a background static like the beating of her heart or the sound of her own breath.

The headphones had a dual purpose, though. Not only did they supply the ambient music with which she has chosen to permeate her life in a near-constant stream, but they served as a kind of talisman to ward off unwelcome advances. Wearing headphones on public transport says, "I couldn't hear you even if I wanted to." They say, "Fuck off. I'm in my own world here and you're not welcome."

Thus armoured, Vanessa turned the rest of her attention to her favourite hobby – people-watching. She didn't stare at people directly. That would be rude and, frankly, dangerous. Instead, she took just fleeting glances off to the side or let her eyes roam about the train carriage in a manner affectedly casual. There were the regulars there, of course. The morning commuters on their way to the office or the shop or wherever it was they performed their daily grind. Vanessa has never spoken to any of them, but she had little narratives in her head for each. There was the middle-aged man with the brightly patterned business shirts who Vanessa imagined was going through some quiet, tepid version of a mid-life crisis. There was the twenty-something-year-old man with the too-shiny shoes that Vanessa imagined was sliming his way up the corporate ladder in whatever business he had, like a parasite, attached himself to. There was the pretty woman with the long chestnut hair who Vanessa mostly just imagined lounging in booths in dimly-lit bars or casting devious looks at her from the other side of her bed.

Vanessa wasn't interested in any of these today, however. She was looking for fresh stimulus. Her roving eye scanned the other passengers in the carriage, looking for some kind of quirk or idiosyncrasy to spark her imagination. The train was relatively quiet today, though. Most people had already started their Christmas holidays and it was too early in the day for shoppers. Disappointed by the limited, and rather mundane, crowd Vanessa was about to give up her game when her eyes met those of a woman in the row of seats diagonally opposite her. Vanessa's heart skipped guiltily, but she forced herself to hold the woman's gaze for a moment longer before looking away. To look away any sooner would seem suspicious.

For several breaths Vanessa turned her gaze outside the window, but her thoughts were still on the woman. When she turned back she found the woman still looking at her. The woman smiled. Vanessa's face burnt but, instead of looking away, she found herself smiling in return. The woman stood up and moved to the seat directly opposite Vanessa. She looked Vanessa in the eye and tapped at her ear with a well-manicured finger. Vanessa lifted her hands up to her headphones then hesitated, reluctant to remove her only safeguard, but the woman's eyes were warm and inviting and Vanessa lowered her headphones, letting them hang loosely around her neck. She could still faintly hear the music as the headphones vibrated gently against her skin.

"What are you listening to?" the woman asked. Her voice was deep but somehow soft. "Queen." Vanessa replied and the woman laughed, "That's more *my* generation's music!" Her laughter was rich. Musical. Vanessa's spine tingled slightly. Vanessa had first assumed the woman to be in her forties or fifties but, after her comment, Vanessa looked a little closer and revised her estimate to mid-sixties. A very fit mid-sixties. The woman began chatting amiably – about the weather (too hot), about her upcoming visit to her parents' place in Mornington (too far away) and about her job, which was something to do with telecommunications (too boring). She didn't seem to expect much from Vanessa in terms of a reply and that suited Vanessa just fine. Vanessa smiled and nodded and uttered the occasional "Oh, really?" as she counted down the stations until her stop.

Suddenly the woman leaned in close and said in a voice so low it was practically a whisper, "What size shoes do you wear?" Vanessa frowned. It was such a personal question but so random that it took her by surprise and she found herself blurting out, "Seven," before she could stop herself.

The woman's face lit up. "I knew it! I just knew it!" she crowed. Vanessa expected the woman to say more by way of an explanation but, instead, she just jumped out of her seat and declared "This is my stop!" then hurried off to the door. They were still several minutes away from the next station but rather than saying anything Vanessa slipped her headphones back on. "Weird," she thought to herself.

*

With the Christmas shopping season well and truly in full swing, Chadstone shopping centre was a bustling hive of activity. Even the boutique record store where

Vanessa worked – a moderately successful business at best – was brimming with customers. Vanessa weaved through a small crowd and made her way behind the counter to the break room. The manager, Rick, was back there already, looking harassed as he unpacked a fresh crate of vinyl. His furrowed brow softened somewhat when he saw Vanessa. "Ah, Ness. You're here. I need to talk to you."

"This can't be good," Vanessa thought, her guard raised. Rick continued, "We've all been flat-out preparing for the extended trading hours and everything's mostly under control..." Vanessa eyed the several unopened boxes of merchandise behind Rick sceptically, "... But I've had something... umm... *personal* come up. I need you to manage the store during the event."

Vanessa's jaw dropped. Every year Chadstone ran an event where the whole shopping centre stayed open for trade for 36 hours, from 6 am on 23 December to 6 pm on Christmas Eve. That was only two days away! In all the years Vanessa had worked there she had only had to work once during the Christmas shopping event and she swore she never would again.

Vanessa chewed on her lower lip, "Rick, I really don't think I can. Not with such short notice."

"You'll get triple-time at the night-manager rate." Rick suddenly declared and Vanessa froze. That was a lot of money. A *whole* lot of money. That might even cover all her Christmas shopping. But, still...

"Do I have a choice?" Vanessa asked. "Not really," Rick replied with surprising candour, "There's no one else."

*

Nick Cave's gravelly voice growled in Vanessa's ears and she glared down at her own feet. She wasn't in the mood for playing her usual game this morning. She had less than twenty-four hours before her nightmare stint as manager of the record store but she had still been called in to work her usual hours today. Her feet tapped, but not in time with the music, just an angry – *thud, thud, thud* as she considered her fate.

Eventually tiring of the view of her own angry feet Vanessa looked up. As with yesterday morning, the train was sparsely populated. Vanessa's eyes were drawn immediately towards a couple that were arguing at the other end of the carriage. The man was tall and probably handsome when he wasn't so angry. The woman was harder to see, her face concealed by long dirty-blonde hair that hang down past her shoulders. In her arms, she was cradling a cardboard box. Vanessa watched the exchange anxiously for a few moments, unsure what to do. With her headphones on Vanessa could not hear what the pair were talking about or even determine if they were yelling or not. "None of my business," she eventually concluded, and she was just about to look away when the woman brushed back her hair and Vanessa felt a sudden jolt of recognition – the woman she met on yesterday morning's train.

Now that she recognised the woman, Vanessa's discomfort increased. Should she intervene? What could she even do? She took a deep breath and pulled back her headphones, only for the man to throw up his arms in defeat, then turn and storm into the next carriage. The woman turned and Vanessa was shocked to see how different she looked than she did yesterday. She seemed beyond tired, as though she had somehow had a whole week's worth of sleepless nights in the one night since Vanessa saw her. As the woman's eyes settled on Vanessa, however, her worn face lit up. Clutching the box close to her chest she charged down the carriage toward Vanessa, beaming manically.

Vanessa returned the smile weakly, wishing there was some escape. When the woman settled into the seat opposite her, Vanessa asked awkwardly, "Are you okay?"

The woman blinked in surprise, then laughed her silvery laugh, "Oh *that*? That was nothing. It's all sorted now." As the woman spoke her long and elegant fingernails tapped at the box she held. Vanessa turned her attention to the box and noticed with some surprise that it was a shoe box. But not just any shoe box, a dun-coloured box with the name 'Christian Louboutin' scrawled across the lid in white script.

The woman was talking again, but Vanessa was not listening. Suddenly the woman stood up and Vanessa jerked back in surprise. "My stop!" the woman cried and Vanessa looked out the window, noting that they were still several stops before the station the woman got off at yesterday. As Vanessa turned back, the woman abruptly shoved the box in at her chest. "This is for you!" she declared as a confused Vanessa accepted the proffered object. "Th-thank you," Vanessa stammered automatically, but the woman had already walked away. The train pulled up at the station and the woman disembarked without so much as a backwards glance at Vanessa.

Vanessa looked down in confusion at the box on her lap, "Weird," she thought, but there was no time to think anything else as she hurried to get off at her stop.

*

Although Vanessa did manage to arrive for work on time (just barely) she spent most of the morning feeling flustered and harried. She didn't even think of the box, which she had stored hastily in the break room when she arrived, until it was time for lunch.

Munching on her salad roll, Vanessa picked up the box with one hand and gave it a tentative shake. It certainly did feel like shoes. Stuffing the last morsel of roll into her mouth, Vanessa lifted the lid. Nestled in a bed of tissue paper was a pair of black high heels with vibrant red soles in size seven.

Vanessa gaped. They couldn't be genuine, surely? Who would give a complete stranger a pair of designer shoes? Vanessa squirmed in her seat. This felt too... intimate. Who was that woman on the train? Some sort of foot fetishist? A slave trader? Or perhaps just her fairy godmother.

The shoes weren't really Vanessa's style but she decided to try them on anyway. She kicked off her trusty Docs and, feeling a little like Cinderella, slipped the high heels on. A perfect fit.

Sarah, Vanessa's co-worker for that shift, stuck her head into the break room "Aren't you finished yet?" she snapped. Vanessa started, then looked at her watch. 12:36. So she had apparently been admiring her own feet for ten whole minutes. Vanessa scoffed at herself, then jumped to her feet and headed back into the store. "Nice shoes." Said Sarah with genuine admiration as Vanessa passed by. Vanessa replied with a distracted grunt as she hurried back to her post.

The rest of the working day went smoothly for Vanessa. Very smoothly, in fact. After a morning of feeling like she was running behind, Vanessa suddenly felt in control. In charge. It was as though the shoes had given her a boost in confidence. "Maybe they're lucky", she thought. "Maybe I'll wear them home."

Walking home from to train station Vanessa was surprised by how comfortable the shoes felt. After wearing them for the whole afternoon at work, standing on the train , and now walking home they felt at least as supportive as her usual shoes and twice as snug. They made a pleasing sound as she walked along, too. Crossing the bridge in her new heels Vanessa felt like one of the three billy-goats gruff: *trip-trap, trip-trap, trip-trap*.

When she got home, Vanessa eyed her familiar slippers askance. She considered leaving her new shoes on, but her fear of scuffing the floors in her rented unit won over and, reluctantly, she slipped the shoes off.

She went to put them away in her bedroom, but they looked so out of place beside the rest of her footwear, most of it thrifted. After much thought, she pulled out the shoe box from her backpack, removed the Docs she had tucked away there, and gently placed the new heels back in their home before placing the box on her bedside table. It was the last thing she saw before falling asleep.

*

Vanessa dreamt of a wide horizon and a sky like inky flesh pierced with diamonds. The ground beneath her heaved and trembled and she looked down to see that she was standing on a path made of living human bodies. As she stepped, her new heels slipped into meat as easily as a key into a padlock, piercing skin and then sinking in deep. Without knowing why, she added a cruel twist and noted how the shoes made a satisfyingly wet noise as she withdrew them. She was vaguely aware of voices, thin and weak, whimpering apologies, pleading for mercy. She knew no mercy, though. All she knew as she made her inexorable advance across this sea of ruined muscle and bone was the imperative to continue and the moist sound of her own progress: *schluck, schluck, schluck.* Somewhere ahead of her someone was waiting. Someone important. Nothing would stop her from reaching the figure that called to her from the distance. Not the writhing, mewling figures beneath her. Not the blood and viscera that made slick her path and stained her soles a deeper, murkier shade of red. Not even that persistent buzzing coming from somewhere off to her left...

... Vanessa woke up groggily to the sound of her phone's alarm. She was vaguely aware of having had a dream... or a nightmare perhaps... but as she rubbed the sleep from her eyes the last lingering threads of what she had seen as she slumbered slipped away leaving only the uneasy sense of something being left incomplete.

As she dragged herself through her morning routine – breakfast, teeth, shower – Vanessa remembered that today was the start of the 36-hour trade. Not an ideal time to be feeling so drowsy. Her mood brightened somewhat when she remembered her new shoes and she immediately went to her bedroom and took them out of their box. They were every bit as beautiful as she remembered. More so, even. She knew immediately that today she must dress with even more care than usual. The shoes deserved it. *Demanded* it.

From the depths of her substantial wardrobe, Vanessa retrieved a sleek, black pencil skirt and, after some consideration, paired it with a silky, crimson dress shirt with a pussy-bow. "Red to match my soles!" Vanessa said to herself, then frowned as a fragment of the previous night's dream flickered across her mind before receding again, just beyond the reach of her consciousness.

On the train heading to work, Vanessa was a little surprised not to see the woman. She was ambivalent about the woman's absence – on the one hand, she was disappointed to not be able to properly thank her benefactor, on the other, she was relieved that she was spared the awkwardness of having to face the stranger who gave her such an extravagant gift. What would she even say?

As she got off at her station, Vanessa noticed a tall figure on the opposite platform – a man in a grey business suit. While the morning crowds all milled about, this figure was so still that he immediately drew Vanessa's eye, though no one else seemed to be troubled by him. He seemed to be staring down, maybe at his own feet or perhaps at the train tracks below. Suddenly he looked up, directly meeting her eyes, and Vanessa was startled to realise that she recognised the man. He was the one who has arguing with the strange lady on the day she gave Vanessa the shoes. She froze under the man's gaze and a slow smile crept across his face. Gradually he lowered his gaze again, raking down her body until he reached her shoes. Vanessa turned and scurried off towards work and, more to the point, away from the tall man.

*

The Christmas shopping event was every bit as harrowing as Vanessa had imagined. She was supposed to get a break every five hours, but even when she did manage to slip off to the break room she barely had time to take a few deep breaths before one of the shop assistants barged in to ask her a question. Vanessa wondered why Rick put the least experienced staff members on during this event, but really she knew the answer – none of the regular staff were stupid enough to take up the offer. None except her. She should complain. She should go to the Fair Work Ombudsman or something. No one should have to work this many hours at a time. Every time she thought this, though, she remembered the amount Rick was paying her, bit her lip, and dove back into work.

At about the halfway mark, at the end of what was technically Vanessa's first of two consecutive shifts, she took her first real break. She left the store and headed to the nearest food court to get herself some dinner.

Four hours. That is how long she had before the start of her next shift. Not long enough to go home and sleep but long enough to be bored out of her mind. She decided to see a movie to pass the time, and ended up dozing intermittently in the plush seats of the cinema while the latest installment in one of the more popular modern movie franchises played out blandly before her. All she was really aware of as she sat slumped in her seat were flashes of contrasting orange and teal.

By the time the credits rolled Vanessa was a zombie – not asleep but not really awake either. The film was about two hours long including trailers and so, mercifully perhaps, Vanessa now only had one more hour to fill before returning to work. She dragged herself through the meandering corridors of Chadstone aimlessly, glancing frequently at her phone and begging for an end to this interminable 'shopping extravaganza' hell. An end to the festive music playing through the loudspeakers throughout the shopping centre. An end to the tinsel and glitter and fake reindeer. An end to the jostling, seething, raucous crowds.

Just then Vanessa realised the crowds *were* gone. She looked about and there was no one around her. Not in any direction. She was alone in this stretch of shops and the only sound, other than the ubiquitous Christmas music, was the sound of her own footsteps on the polished floor – *click-clack, click-clack, click-clack.*

What's more, she didn't even recognise where in Chadstone she was. Sure, there was the Kate Spade store, but wasn't that supposed to be next to Hugo Boss, not Lacoste? And where was the Apple store? And... wait... was that just Kate Spade she passed again?

Vanessa slowed down and raised a hand to her temple. She must just be tired. Sometimes things don't seem right when you're tired, right? If she just kept going she was bound to end up somewhere she recognised, or somewhere that wasn't deserted at least.

As Vanessa walked on she fixed her gaze directly in front of herself and tried not to notice the shops that seemed to repeat themselves in an endless loop on either side of her. Finally, with a rush of excitement, Vanessa was able to make out some sort of figure in the previously featureless walkway. She sped up.

"Hello!" Vanessa called out to the figure, "Can you help me, please?".

The figure made no response and just stood immobile. For a moment Vanessa feared it was just a mannequin taken from one of the stores but as she got closer recognition began to dawn. It was the man. The man from the train station. At the precise moment that Vanessa made this realisation, the Christmas music cut out, and she was plunged into a sudden and unfamiliar silence.

Behind the man, the lights of the shopping centre cut out. He began to walk towards Vanessa, and as he passed each light fixture it flicked off, so that it was like he was dragging a cloak of sheer darkness behind him.

Vanessa turned and ran, but what was the point? It was like being on a treadmill. She ran and ran but makes no progress. The same four or five shops on either side whizzed past her again and again.

Suddenly there was a hand on her shoulder. Exhausted and defeated, Vanessa stopped and let out a weak sob. She turned and found the man looking down at her, a soft smile on his lips and a sympathetic look in his beautiful, dark eyes.

"Why were you running?" he asked. Vanessa was too tired to think of anything but the truth, "I was scared."

"You don't need to be scared of me, Vanessa," the man said in a voice soft like velvet, "We can be friends you and I." The man's tone was lilting. Hypnotic, almost. Vanessa felt her eyes droop even as she stood there.

"We have so much in common, after all. The shoes, for one thing..."

"M-my shoes?" Vanessa gazed down at her feet in bleary confusion.

"Ah-ah!" the man gently admonished, waving a finger at her, "*Our* shoes. They may be yours during the day, but every night, just for a couple of hours, they belong to me. You may still wear them, but they do what I say."

Vanessa's head swam. She didn't know what the man was talking about. She was too tired to make any sense of this and, besides, it must almost be time for her next shift.

"I have to go to work," she mumbled.

"Yes, you do." The man replied as he gently took her elbow and guided her to one of the plush sofas sitting in the middle of the walkway. "It *does* look comfortable," Vanessa thought as she slid into the cushy seat. The man sat beside her and lowered her head into his lap, "Maybe I'll just close my eyes for a moment."

*

It was Christmas Eve and Vanessa felt like she hadn't slept at all. As she sat on the train, her head lolling limply to one side, she tried to replay the past thirty-six hours over in her head, but it all bled together and she couldn't quite distinguish what actually happened from what she saw in the movie and what she dreamt when she nodded off between shifts.

Her shoes no longer felt as comfortable as when she first tried them on. They felt too tight and pinched her toes. All she could think about was getting home and kicking them off. She kept nodding off, but every time she did she woke up with a start. She was so tired but for some reason, she just didn't feel safe sleeping, even though the carriage was empty.

Well, not entirely empty. "I *love* your shoes!" gushed a girl in her early twenties. Vanessa was so drowsy she had not even noticed the young woman, even though she was directly opposite her. "Thanks," mumbled Vanessa.

The young woman was dressed neatly in a crisp suit. Taking the train this late on Christmas Eve Vanessa thought that perhaps, like her, the girl worked in retail. Or perhaps she has an office job and was running close to a deadline...

...Vanessa shook her head and stopped herself before she began making up stories in her head. Whether the woman was a shop assistant or a high-flying executive or something else entirely, didn't really matter. Nothing really did anymore.

"I really wish I could afford shoes like that," sighed the girl. Vanessa looked the young woman in the face.

She could be anyone, really, but it was better that, to Vanessa at least, she just remain a no-one.

Vanessa smiled weakly at the girl, then asked, as casually as she could manage, "You wouldn't happen to be a size seven?"

CHRISTMAS IN JULY

DARRIEL PULLED DOWN HER BEANIE and tightened her scarf so that barely a single freckle on her face was peeping out of the gap between them. She slammed the door of her car (an old bomb she'd bought to serve her for the length of her stay) a little harder than was strictly necessary.

This wasn't the way things were supposed to be at all. When she'd first decided to move to Australia, she had pictured sunny days and sandy beaches. She'd never really given any thought to what the winters would be like. A friend of hers had spent a year up at the Gold Coast and had gushed about the warm weather year-round and Darriel had just assumed it would be the same everywhere. But Victoria was a world apart from Queensland and Darriel was surprised to be met with a winter almost as cold as those back home in New York. There were beaches here, alright, but no one told her there the beaches would be populated by *penguins*!

What made matters worse is that there was nothing to look forward to in the cooler months here in Australia. Fall (or *autumn* as people kept correcting her) had passed without Halloween or Thanksgiving or pumpkin-spiced anything! Now she found herself mired in the middle of a winter without even the promise of Christmas to look forward to.

When Ross and Jess had extended an invitation to her to join them for dinner at their home in the Dandenongs a morose Darriel had almost refused. She didn't really feel in the mood for driving out to the mountains and meeting new people but, then again, she had nothing better to do.

The Rue's home was a rustic brick house, but *big*. Bigger than Darriel had expected, although she supposed that was probably why they had chosen to live so far away from the city. The plot of land it was on was big, too. Darriel could see a thick expanse of trees behind the house, but she couldn't see how far back it extended. It was like Ross and Jess had their own private slice of the bush.

TWELVE NIGHTS

Darriel rang the doorbell and could vaguely hear a chiming coming from deep within the house. As she waited for the response Darriel shivered and stomped her feet. She thought about her apartment or, more accurately, of the hot water bottle and fluffy robe she kept in her bedroom.

Suddenly the door was flung open and Ross, beaming at Darriel through salt-and-pepper whiskers, announced, "Merry Christmas!"

Darriel pulled back a little and blinked in confusion. "Wh-what?" she stammered. She looked over her host's shoulder and saw that inside was bright and welcoming and, well, *jolly*. As she stepped inside Ross handed her a mug of a familiar-smelling liquid. Darriel took a sip. Eggnog!

"Come meet the others!" Ross insisted, placing a hand on the small of Darriel's back to guide her further into loungeroom, where a wood fire was crackling merrily in the hearth. "I must be dreaming," Darriel thought, unravelling her scarf.

Jess was standing close to the fire talking to a couple who had their backs to Darriel. Jess smiled and waved as Darriel moved closer. "Darriel! This is Benjamin and Lori Taylor. They're from the States, too. Guys, this is Darriel Daniels."

The couple turned and it was only then that Darriel noticed how tall the man was. About six foot. His wife (or so Darriel assumed her to be) was much shorter, closer to Darriel's height. Darriel smiled shyly, "Hi," she murmured softly.

"Well, hi there!" responded Benjamin in his Northwest accent. Darriel's smile faltered a little but she quickly recovered from her disappointment. East Coast or West, it was nice to hear another American accent for a change.

Beside the couple, Darriel could see a row of woollen stockings hung along the mantelpiece, bringing her thought back to the peculiar situation she had entered. "So, what exactly is going on here?" she asked, taking another sip of her eggnog.

"It's Christmas in July!" exclaimed Ross, joining the others by the fireside. Darriel did not feel any more enlightened. "It's an old tradition," explained Jess, "Because so many Australians originally came from the UK and the rest of Europe, we like to have a pretend Christmas celebration in the middle of winter to remind us of the Christmases 'back home'."

"Oh," responded Darriel contemplatively, then she brightened, "Actually that's a really fun idea!"

"We thought our yank friends might be missing the winters back in their own home, so we decided to invite you here to celebrate." Jess expanded.

"So... What exactly happens at 'Christmas in July'," asked Darriel.

"Everything that happens at regular Christmas" responded Ross, "Only colder".

"I'll just go see how Matt is getting on with the dinner." Announced Jess, excusing herself from the group.

"You have a lovely home, Ross," said Lori.

"Thanks, we put a lot of work into it. Well, Jess put a lot of work into it. I can show you guys the rest of the property after dinner, if you'd like."

"How big *is* the property," Darriel asked "From the front it looked like it extended back a fair way."

"Oh, pretty big," replied Ross evasively. "But, here, let me show you through to the dining room."

The dining room was a long, narrow space with fairy lights strung up and down its length. Dominating the room was a big timber table that looked like it belonged in a boarding school or monastery. The table was all laid out for dinner with elegant place settings accented with bright Christmas crackers. The centrepiece of the whole affair was a spray of tinsel and baubles. Right at the centre of the display was a small, silver bell. Darriel leaned in for a closer inspection and saw that the handle of the bell was decorated with the form of a koala and joey. The more Darriel looked at the bell, the less she liked it. There was something oddly disproportionate about the koalas.

Darriel was still looking at the bell when Jess entered the room from the kitchen, reached for the bell and rang it briskly. "Dinner is ready!" she announced.

Ross' father, Matt, came in bearing trays of roasted meat and vegetables. There was even turkey, Darriel saw with delight. Well, turkey breast, anyway. Everyone took their places at the table and chatted happily as they passed the dishes around and served themselves. Once everyone had filled their own plates Ross cried, "Time for bon-bons!" and held aloft the Christmas cracker that had been sitting on his bread plate. Ross and Jess tugged at either side of the cracker and it burst, spitting out a small package consisting of a paper crown wrapped around a tiny plastic frog. Ross wasted no time in donning the crown. As he did so a little slip of paper fell out. Ross unravelled the paper and read aloud, "What do they sing at a snowman's birthday party?" The company deliberated for some time but could not come up with a response. "Freeze a jolly good fellow!" Ross declared. Matt laughed and everyone else groaned.

"Are they all that good?" asked Benjamin. "Of course!" Jess replied, "Check it out," and at that, she picked up her own Christmas cracker and turned to Lori to offer her the other end. When they pulled the novelty apart with a bang, Jess was left holding the larger share. She reached inside the cardboard tube and withdrew her own package, putting on the paper crown and tossing aside the plastic toy with distaste. She read her joke, "Where do hundreds-and-thousands come from?" Again, everyone was stumped. Jess pulled a face as she read the answer, "They're Smarties poo."

Darriel couldn't help but chuckle at that one. It was so bad it was good. Benjamin eagerly picked up his own cracker and turned to Lori to pull it apart. He hastily put on the crown, then searched about the debris for the joke. He found the slip of paper and held it up triumphantly before lowering it so he could read it. His smile quickly faded.

"What's wrong?" asked Lori.

"*Winter is much like unrequited love; cold and merciless,*" Benjamin read in a stiff monotone. Everyone fell silent as they considered this. It was Lori who eventually spoke, "I suppose it's like fortune cookies? Some of them are just quotes?"

"Let's try yours, Lori," suggested Matt, reaching towards her. Lori picked up her cracker and there was the usual bang. Lori searched through the bon-bon's scattered remains for the slip of paper. "'*Nothing burns like the cold'*... Well, I suppose not."

"Come on, Darriel," urged Jess from her seat opposite, "Let's see if you got a joke or a dud."

Darriel eyed her cracker warily. She had found the quotes in the other guest's crackers vaguely unsettling and had an uneasy feeling about what her own might say. Still, by this point everyone had fallen silent and were watching curiously and so, reluctantly, Darriel picked up her cracker and proffered the other end to Jess. Darriel squeezed her eyes tight as they pulled it apart, then peeked out to look at the ensuing mess. From the carcass of the cracker, Darriel withdrew the paper crown and donned it solemnly before reaching for the small piece of paper. It read simply, "*Don't look up.*"

Instinctively everyone glanced at the ceiling. From the other end of the table Lori squealed, causing Darriel to jump and whip her head around. As she did, though, she saw that the other woman was smiling. When Darriel looked at the ceiling above Lori she saw suspended a small spring of mistletoe.

"Merry Christmas, love," said Matt, leaning in to peck Lori on the cheek. "Hey! What about me?" asked Benjamin, feigning offence, and Lori laughed as she turned to place a placating kiss on her husband's lips.

Darriel was smiling now, too. It seemed she had got the best joke out of everyone. It was a clever trick her hosts had played and Darriel, deciding to keep her piece of paper as a memento, folded it carefully and slipped it into her purse.

After dinner, the group gathered around the fireplace and digested. "I've had an elegant sufficiency," Matt proclaimed, patting his belly with satisfaction. He drew closer to the fire and raised up his hands to warm them. In the glow of the firelight, his eyebrows furrowed, "You lot are lucky. Yanks handle the cold better. Us Aussies hate the winter."

"It's not so bad!" Benjamin admonished, "It's the summers here that really get me."

"Sure, summer can be harsh and relentless and a little, well... *on fire*... but winter is lonely and... *hungry*," Matt said grimly.

"I guess that's why we're here!" piped up Lori.

Though usually the most effusive of the group, Matt didn't respond. He just continued to stare at the fire sombrely.

Ross tried to break the awkward silence, "You know, in the old days in England it used to be traditional to tell ghost stories on Christmas Eve."

Jess scoffed, "There're no ghosts here!"

"Just the drop bear," offered Matt.

"What's a drop bear?" Darriel asked. Lori laughed and Benjamin rolled his eyes and responded wearily, "It's just a joke Aussies play on tourists. It isn't real."

"Oh, but it *is* real!" insisted Jess, "It's like a koala but bigger and meaner and carnivorous. It catches its prey by dropping out of the highest tree branches."

"Its body is kind of flat," added Ross, "So it can control its descent. It doesn't have a mouth on its head, instead it has a big gaping maw right in the middle of its torso..."

Darriel laughed at this, "No animals have mouths in their *torso*! Not land animals, anyway."

"It's not really an animal, as such," explained Ross, "It's more like a spirit. It's been here forever."

"And how long is forever?" asked Benjamin in a mocking tone, "It's not like Australia has been here that long."

"The *English* only came to Australia in the late 1700s, and we didn't become a federation until 1901, but Aboriginal Australians constitute probably the world's longest continuous living culture. At least 60,000 years they've been here."

The group considered this for a moment. Darriel tried but failed to imagine anything stretching back that far. It was Lori who broke the silence "So I guess that makes you guys newcomers, too?"

Matt smiled at this "You're not wrong, love. We're living on borrowed land here. Well, stolen, really. We owe an immeasurable debt to this country, one which we've so far avoided paying."

"The drop bear knows, though," pressed Ross. "It knows what belongs here and what doesn't. It usually leaves people alone," he paused dramatically, then continued with a smirk, "But it's attracted by foreign accents."

"Luckily I've been working on my Aussie." Benjamin said then, straightening up in his seat, lets out a careful, drawn-out, "Gee-Day!".

The Australians ignored this. Jess leaned in close to the group and said, almost in a whisper, "The weirdest thing about the drop bear is that even though it lives at the very top of trees, even though its prey is always below, it's always looking... up," as she said this she sat back in her chair again and let her eyes roll back in her head so that only the whites were showing. With the fire casting shadows on her face from below the effect of her expression was somewhat startling, but the Americans were unimpressed.

"Bullshit!" insisted Benjamin.

There was a brief, tense silence before both Ross and Jess burst out laughing, "Okay, okay, you've got us. It's just a little joke of ours..." admitted Jess.

"...That you'll forgive, we hope." finished Ross, "We wouldn't really be Australian if we didn't at least *try* to convince you of drop bears."

In the comfortable silence that followed, Darriel turned back to the fire. Her belly was full, her body was warm and she was in good company. *It really is like Christmas*; she thought with a smile.

"There is one more Christmas tradition we haven't tried yet," Matt offered, breaking the quiet. "Carols by candlelight."

"Oh!" cried Lori, "We do that in the States, too! Could we really do it?"

Jess grinned, "Of course! We have plenty of candles and the perfect place out back to go and sing. It's beautiful and deep enough in the trees that we won't disturb the neighbours."

"As if my singing ever disturbed anyone!" Matt feigned offence before bursting into song, "Si-lent night! Ho-oly night!...."

The off-key and impressively loud rendition caused Darriel to jump and pulled her attention away from the fire.

"Yeah..." Benjamin said, "Maybe a secluded location is a good idea."

"I'll go grab the candles!" said Jess, leaping out of her seat. The others followed, chatting and laughing merrily. Darriel lagged behind, reluctant to leave the warmth and comfort of her current place. She took one last longing look at the fire just as the largest log split in the heat and sent a spray of sparks shooting up the chimney.

*

The group huddled close together, their collective breaths steaming in the cold air. It was not very late, but it was already dark. Darker than Darriel, who lived close to the city, was used to. The only light the group brought with them was the candles that Jess had gathered with

39

them. Benjamin had asked if they should bring a torch as well, but Jess had insisted that this would ruin the effect and that the candles were sufficient. She had brought two extra boxes of matches just in case.

The back of Ross and Jess' property did indeed seem to be a patch of bushland, dense and fragrant with eucalyptus oil. "How far back does it go?" asked Darriel. "Oh... a-ways." Ross responded vaguely.

Although they had been chatting and laughing as they initially prepared to go out, now as they passed the line of trees and entered the bushland silence fell once more upon the group. After almost a minute trudging along Darriel finally asked, "So... when do we start singing?"

"Not yet," replied Jess, "We have to get there first." Her voice sounded tense to Darriel, but she wasn't sure whether she was just projecting her own anxieties.

Darriel's nerves were not helped when, after another few silent minutes, Benjamin let out an ear-splitting shout, "Tarantula!"

A visibly shaken Benjamin prepared to squash the spider, but as he raised his leg Matt roared, "STOP!"

Benjamin froze, then slowly lowered his leg, allowing the large spider to escape. "That's a huntsman," explained Matt, "We don't kill them".

"Are you serious?" Benjamin barked back, "That thing was *huge*! Why wouldn't you kill it?"

"They don't do us any harm." Matt insisted, "And they kill pests".

Benjamin muttered something under his breath that Darriel couldn't make out. She was beginning to regret accepting this invitation after all.

The group trudged on, Darriel stomping her feet as they progressed in an attempt to keep warm. Darriel was about to ask about their progress when she was interrupted by a horrendous noise from above. It was a hissing, shrieking noise and Darriel's blood ran cold. She did not know what it was, but it sounded like a cat fighting with a giant snake.

"Just a possum," Jess stated calmly.

In the dim light of the candles, Darriel couldn't quite make out the expressions on her companions' faces. She wondered if her fellow Americans were as rattled as she. She thought it unlikely until she heard Lori cry in a strangled voice, "What is *that*?" Lori pointed to the branches above and Darriel followed her finger, seeing nothing at first until she raised her candle and the light reflected off a pair of beady eyes up high in the branches. The thing in the trees stirred, then suddenly dove out, causing both Darriel and Lori to shriek.

"Calm down," Ross urged, "It's just a fruit bat."

Instinctively, Darriel's free hand flew up to protect her face and hair.

"That was a bat?" Lori asked, sounding even more shaken than Darriel felt. "I've seen *cats* smaller than that!"

Darriel had to agree. The thing was huge. As it flew away, she could hear the leathery beat of its wings in the air.

"They don't call them megabats for nothing," Ross replied, and Darriel fancied she heard a derisive tone in his voice. This certainly wasn't turning out to be the jolly, Christmassy activity that was promised.

The further the group progressed into the bush the darker it became. Night was advancing and the cover of the trees became more dense until they finally reached a spot where the trees blocked out most of the moonlight.

It was eerily quiet here, but Darriel could see how it might be good for singing. She thought with relief that this must be the place they had been looking for. As if reading her thoughts Jess announced, "We're here."

"It's beautiful," said Lori. "What I can see of it, that is."

The surroundings became suddenly darker as all three Australians snuffed out their candles.

"Hey! What's the idea?" shouted Benjamin "I can barely see!"

There was no response save for the sound of footsteps retreating.

"Ross? Jess?" Lori asked weakly, but it was Matt who responded.

"Sorry guys, it's nothing personal. Winter is lean times and appetites have to be satisfied."

"What the fuck!?" Benjamin shouted out and he turned around to try and see where their friends had gone, but that had already escaped the meagre reach of his feeble candle. He risked losing even that as he frantically spun about. Darriel found herself cradling her own light protectively.

From somewhere now quite distant, Ross' voice floated back to the Americans, "Maybe... don't look up."

And with that the Australians were gone, leaving their guests stranded in dense bushland somewhere at the back of their property.

"Okay... okay..." began Benjamin, sounding most assuredly *not* okay, "It's just another one of their dumb Aussie jokes. But we still have our candles. We'll be fine to make it out again as long as we don't—"

From above came a low, guttural grunt. The three froze. Lori eventually managed to whisper, "What was that?" to which Darriel suggested optimistically, "A... possum?"

The grunt came again, louder now. Darriel could see Benjamin and Lori huddling close together about six feet away from her. She was contemplating moving closer when something dropped from the bush canopy above the couple.

Darriel could not quite make out the form of the thing except that it was large and furry. As it fell its glowing eyes left a streak of after-images in the air – a whole trail of eyes, all looking upwards.

As the thing descended on Benjamin and Lori it seemed to unfold on itself and Lori could now make out large ears and an impossibly large mouth. The couple screamed in unison as the thing hit them with a wet thud.

Darriel let out a strangled gasp and turned to flee, but in the dark she tripped up on a tree root. Pain shot up from her ankle and she fell to her knees, her candle snuffing out as she fell. In the dense bush, without a light and now with a twisted or broken ankle there was nowhere for Darriel to run. Somewhere behind her, she could hear the wet sounds of the thing chewing on Benjamin...or maybe Lori.

For the first time since her childhood, Darriel found herself appealing to a higher power. The words she choked out through sobs of fear were a jumbled mixture of vaguely-remembered childhood prayers and her own desperate entreaties for salvation or mercy.

She persisted with this for several minutes even after the noises of the others' grisly, shared demise had ceased. As Darriel listened to the rustling of the eucalyptus overhead a sense of calm acceptance of her fate washed over her. She knew, then, with a kind of detached clarity that the response to her prayers would come from somewhere above.

TWELVE NIGHTS

KATHERINE KITCHENER

THERE'S NO SUCH THING

MAY SIGHED WITH RELIEF as she lowered her weary body to the side of the bed. Slowly, feeling every muscle and joint in her body protest, she shuffled herself into position and slid her legs between the sheets.

"I'd forgotten how tiring it can be running after a child," she breathed as she propped up her pillow and settled herself against it.

"It's been a long time," replied Graham, not looking up from his book.

May and Graham's son Peter and his wife and child were visiting from the eastern states for Christmas. May had spent the whole day taking care of her grandchild,

Jacob, while Peter and his wife travelled to the nearest city to do some last-minute Christmas shopping.

That was the one downside about May and Graham's idyllic property in the West Australian outback. It was a half-hour drive to the nearest town, which had precious few amenities itself, and to get any *real* shopping done the only viable option was to travel to Mandurah, over two hours away. When Peter and Helen had gone out to buy Jacob's Christmas presents they decided to make a day of it so as to make the round-trip worthwhile.

Graham put his book down and took his glasses off. "I don't know why they left it so late," he grumbled. "It's Christmas Eve! It must be chaos out there."

"They didn't want Jacob to find the presents," May reminded him, "He's getting to that age where he's curious and prone to snoop. It would be such a shame to ruin the magic when he's only four years old."

May became misty-eyed as she remembered her son at that age "I'll never forget the wonder in Peter's eyes on Christmas morning when he woke up to a pillowcase full of presents from Santa."

"That's one thing you haven't forgotten at least." Graham responded a little gruffly, but then he turned to May and smiled, squeezing her hand, "It's good to remember those days."

The couple sat in companionable silence for some time before May asked, "How *did* you manage to hide the Christmas gifts from Peter?"

At this, Graham laughed, "Your mind is playing tricks on you again, love. You were the one who organised Peter's Christmas presents."

May frowned, "No, that isn't right... is it? I bought Peter's Christmas present from *us*, but you arranged all the presents from *Santa*."

Graham shook his head firmly. "No, that wasn't me."

Confused, May sat and tried to concentrate on those memories, methodically going back through the years right up to Peter's first Christmas in 1985. A creeping sense of dread trickled through May's body. She was so sure she hadn't bought Peter's Christmas presents herself, had no memory of placing them under the tree... but who did? Out here in the middle of nowhere (or near enough to) who else even could have?

As if reading her thoughts Graham suggested, "Perhaps it was Santa Claus?"

"Don't tease!" snapped May, hating how thin and querulous her voice sounded to her own ears, "I hate it when you tease." Graham just laughed softly.

That feeling of dread settled firmly in May's chest, tugging at her heart. She suddenly felt that she couldn't possibly sleep. "I'm going to wait up for Peter," she announced.

"Don't be like that," Graham cajoled, "You're just misremembering things again, that's all. Come back to bed."

"What? No, that's not it," May lied, "I'm just worried about Peter and Eileen. I want to see that they get home safe."

Graham grunted at this. "Alright then, love. Just try not to wake me when you come back to bed. Early morning, tomorrow." He rolled over and almost immediately began to snore. The tightness in May's chest loosened somewhat.

May padded out to the living room in her fuzzy slippers. She stood there indecisively for a moment before creeping up to the room next to hers and Graham's and opening the door ever so carefully. The curtain in this room was open and the moonlight streamed through illuminating the form of her slumbering four-year-old grandson. May smiled softly as she watched the steady rise and fall of Jacob's back as he lay belly first on the bed that used to be his father's. May's heart swelled with love and pride. She couldn't believe how much Jacob had grown. It seemed like only a moment ago he was a newborn. In fact, it didn't really seem like that long since Peter himself had been this age. The thought brought a tinge of sadness to her mood and her smile faltered somewhat as she gently closed the door and moved back to the loungeroom.

Shuffling up to the sofa, May made sure to turn on the lamp rather than the room light so as not to disturb Graham or Jacob. She settled into her usual spot with a sound somewhere between a wheeze and a sigh. Why was it that she didn't seem to be able to do anything these days without an accompanying sound breaking forth unintended and unwanted? How long had things been like this? When had she become – *old*?

May picked up the magazine that was sitting beside her but almost immediately put it down again listlessly. She cast her eyes around the room and they settled on the Christmas tree, its little yellow lights twinkling merrily. The base of the tree was cluttered with wrapped gifts and right up front and centre was Jacob's still-empty Santa sack that he had placed out with such excitement several hours ago before May settled him for bed. May thought again of her conversation with Graham a few minutes earlier.

"Perhaps my mind *is* slipping," she mused unhappily, "The rest of me seems to be, anyway." As she thought this, May found herself starting to doze.

*

Her dreams always began the same way – abstract and fragmented. Images and sounds flashed through her consciousness so frantically that she was never able to grasp onto any one thing, certainly not long enough to be able to remember when she awoke. Gradually, though, the dream seemed to choose its form and crystallise. Tonight, May dreamt of this very house. Not the way it was now – all decked out in its Christmas finery – but the way it was when she was a child living there with her own parents. As with most dreams of her childhood, it was a happy one. She dreamt of her father picking her up and spinning her through the air when he returned from his farm chores. She dreamt of her mother's apple and rhubarb pie and of standing on tip-toes at the kitchen bench to watch as her mother neatly crimped the edges of the pastry with her worn but still deft fingers. There were no siblings to dream of, of course, but there was a seemingly endless stream of cats – Snowball, Gretchen, Rugby and all the others – each making a brief but touching appearance, all remembered fondly. She dreamed also of her dearest friend who had once lived there, too. Her happy friend with all his arms for hugging and his wrinkled, jolly face so big it seemed to fill up the entire room as he smiled and smiled and smiled...

*

TWELVE NIGHTS

May awoke with a start and with one name on her lips, "Mr Spindle," she whispered reverently. How long had it been since she had last thought of her old imaginary friend? She hadn't forgotten though, she realised with a kind of pride. He'd been waiting for her all this time at the very edge of her subconscious.

She got up to make herself a cup of tea.

The kitchen had changed since she was a child, but perhaps not as much as one might expect. The benches and cabinets were all the same, and although they had installed a new gas oven some twenty years ago or so, the old wood-fire stove still occupied its place against the back wall. Sometimes, on cold winter days, they would light it to warm the place up. It was hot and muggy tonight, of course, so the wood stove remained cold and empty. May lay a hand tenderly on its surface as she waited for the kettle to boil.

That's where Mr Spindle had lived. Behind the oven.

May had been a lonely child, with no siblings of her own and no other children at all within a reasonable distance. She had cats, but cats weren't always the warmest of companions, especially for a young child. And so she had invented Mr Spindle.

Mr Spindle was big and friendly and smelled like cinnamon toast. He had a huge round face. In fact, he was mostly face, with only a stick of a body – much like a very young child's drawing of a person. He could make himself flat like a picture, too. He would shrink himself down and fold himself up so that he fit neatly in the narrow gap between the stove and the wall.

May made her cup of tea and sat down at the kitchen table, all while looking at the old oven.

These days, May often found that memories did not come easily. She had to focus carefully, to ease facts and forms out of the tangled mass of her own mind. And even when she was sure of herself Graham often insisted she was wrong. After her dream, though, the memories of Mr Spindle came, if not flooding back, then at least trickling like a crystal clear creek.

May remembered, for instance, that she used to write letters to Mr Spindle. Well, perhaps 'write' was generous, as she did not even know how to read at the time, but she would scribble on bits of paper. When she was sure her mother wasn't looking she would open up the door to the oven and slip the notes into the fire.

Mr Spindle would sometimes leave her gifts in return. She would reach behind the oven and find some gum nuts or scraps of paperbark. The shimmering feather of a satin bower bird. Sometimes there were even small toys – little dolls made from wooden clothes pegs, a tiny teddy bear. May frowned a little at this memory. Where had the gifts come from? She could imagine putting the things from the garden there herself, even if she could not remember doing so, but what about the toys?

It must have been her mother, she decided. Her mother must have noticed her playing around at the back of the stove and decided to join the game. This didn't feel quite right. Her mother had been a serious, though loving, woman and not given to whimsy. In fact, May had the sense that had she known May was messing around the stove she would have gotten a stern talking to. Could she really have been hiding a lighter side all along?

It *must* have been her mother. Or perhaps it was her father? May sighed heavily. Perhaps she really was losing her memory.

She tapped her fingernails absently upon the kitchen table and gradually the tapping became a tune. May started to hum until, eventually, words came:

> "Mr Spindle is neat as a pin;
> "He has a great, big, funny grin;
> "Mr Spindle lives behind the stove;
> "He is very, very, VERY old;
> "Mr Spindle brings me gifts and toys;
> "He does not even have a voice;
> "Mr Spindle is my dearest friend;
> "He'll be there with me at the end"

May chuckled softly to herself. Why was it there always seemed to be a macabre tinge to the imagination of children? Were they even aware of it? Was *she* when she sang the made-up song happily to herself as a child?

May looked at the kitchen clock as she drained the dregs of her tea. Past midnight and still no sign of Peter and Eileen. She had waited up for four hours now, if you excused the period when she had dozed off. Anxiety tugged at May's chest, but she chastised herself. "He's a grown man. He can look after himself."

She shuffled back into the loungeroom and settled herself once more on the couch. May watched the lights on the tree as they flickered on and off in a series of repeating patterns. Despite the nap and the tea, she still felt drowsy. Her eyelids drooped, and she hovered at the very precipice of sleep.

A loud click startled May out of her dozy state. "The door!" she thought as she heaved herself up off the couch, "Finally!".

Peter had his own keys, of course, but May wanted to meet her son at the door. She was already smiling as she turned the latch and swung open the wooden door. She was greeted, however, by nothing but the muggy, summer night.

May frowned and peered out into the darkness. No car. But she was so sure she heard them arriving.

Disappointed and a little disoriented, May closed the door. As she turned to make her way back to the loungeroom she heard that clicking sound again – a little louder and followed swiftly by a series of other clicks and taps. The sound was coming from inside, she realised.

"Something must have gotten in," May thought resignedly. Out here there were plenty of critters and creepy crawlies who did, unfortunately, have a way of making it into the house every now and then.

Beside the Christmas tree ,a broom was propped up to sweep away the stray needles. May grabbed it and, so armed, headed off to try and track the source of the clicking.

The hallway was empty. No clicking there. She opened her bedroom door but the only noise she found there was Graham's soft snoring. May approached the sewing room, where Jacob was sleeping in his father's old bed. She decided against opening the door and instead pressed an ear to the thin wood and listened. Nothing.

May let out a little huff of frustration and decided to give up and return to the loungeroom. As she made her way back she heard the noise again coming from a little further up the hallway. The kitchen.

May left the light out as she entered the kitchen. She didn't want whatever had broken into the house to scuttle off under the fridge before she has a chance to get at it. Besides, the tree lights in the adjoining loungeroom gave off sufficient, if inconsistent, lighting for her to make her way.

May's eyes swept the room as she entered – running along the skirting boards, around the window frames and even across the ceiling. She sniffed and was met with a smell like slightly burnt toast. Surely she hadn't left the toaster on? She looked at the kitchen bench and saw the toaster, inert and tucked safely away. May's heart began to pound as the smell intensified. Could it be a stroke? Is this really how it all happens?

She could hear the clicking noise still, but it no longer held her attention. Frantically, her eyes flickered to the gas stove – also off – before finally alighting on the old wood-fired oven.

May froze. Something familiar but impossible was creeping out of the space behind the oven. A number of limbs – too many, too long and with too many joints – seemed to unfold out of the shadows. They clicked and creaked as they stretched further out into the kitchen. Each limb ended in a kind of pincer and each pincer held tight in its grip – a toy?

A fluffy teddy bear, a tiny train set, even some sort of hand-held gaming device – the thing somehow dragged them all out of the tiny space between the oven and the wall. As May looked at the toys she noticed that none of them seemed quite whole. The teddy bear was missing an arm and from the unfinished seam at its side hung strands of an oddly iridescent thread. The same threads hung from the other toys. Even the gaming device seemed to be somehow unravelling from the back, where the batteries should go.

Gradually, the thing behind the stove revealed more of itself. An eye the size of a basketball peeked out of the shadows as the thing slowly revealed its body, which really *was* just an enormous, wrinkled head. Its huge, broad mouth was twisted into a manic grin, so wide it seemed to almost encircle the thing's entire head. Its teeth chattered and lips flapped in a parody of speech, but no sound came out but for the *click, click, click* as the teeth met. More of those glimmering threads hung in loops from between the huge, blunt teeth.

The flesh of the thing, both on its immense head and covering its many, many arms, appeared plush and velvety which in combination with the wrinkles made May think, incongruously, of a pug. Except, where puppies wriggled and wagged this thing seemed to vibrate slightly, its whole body shivering in little spasms. Up and down. Up and down.

As the thing advanced, the burnt-toast smell became stronger, undercut now with something sweet and spicy, like cinnamon doughnuts or gingerbread.

May could taste the sickly combination at the back of her throat.

Somewhere inside May, something broke. As she clutched her chest, ambivalence reigned in her racing heart. She was terrified, of course, but also strangely triumphant. Gasping, she fell to her knees and in that moment realised two things with perfect clarity – her memory was as sharp as it had ever been, and there was no such thing as Santa Claus.

TWELVE NIGHTS

KATHERINE KITCHENER

DIRTY DISHES

LEANNE STARED INTO the grey, soapy dishwater and wondered if it was time to refill the sink again. It felt like she had been here forever, washing an endless supply of dishes, but she supposed that is just what it is like when you had the whole family over for Christmas. The McKean family always had a huge Christmas lunch – roast pork with crackling, rolled turkey breast and a huge leg of ham, not to mention all the various vegetables and sides. This year it had been Leanne's turn to host, never mind that she was seven months pregnant. And why was it that, even when she had cooked the entire meal herself, she *still* ended up being the one to do the dishes? It must have been something to do with being the youngest, or the only female among four siblings. At least her mother was here, too, drying the dishes and keeping Leanne company.

The door to the dining room swung open and the sounds of revelry spilled into the kitchen. Leanne didn't even have to turn around to picture the scene – her brothers in their paper crowns, all flushed from too much wine and beer, the various nieces and nephews all playing with their new toys, too engrossed in the novelty of it all to squabble for now. Auntie Cathy breezed in from the dining room, laughing from some aside Leanne had not heard. She was carrying another stack of dirty plates and serving dishes. "That's the last of them!" Cathy declared before spinning around and disappearing back into the celebrations.

"Finally!" Leanne sighed then, when her mother made no response, gave a little laugh to indicate that she was just kidding, after all. "It's been a lovely day," Leanne posited, as much to fill in the silence as anything else. "The kids certainly seem to be enjoying themselves with all their new toys."

"Oh yes!" her mother finally replied, "A few too many toys perhaps, but who can resist spoiling the little things?"

"Christmas is for kids, I guess," Leanne replied.

TWELVE NIGHTS

"So true!" her mother agreed, "Christmas just isn't the same without little ones and Santa and all that. Still, toys today are so strange! I'll never understand Ginny's fascination with those little bug-eyed dolls... what are they called again?"

Leanne laughed, "No idea! But they're hideous, aren't they? I remember when she was still into ponies."

"Oh, that was at least three crazes ago now, Leanne. Keep up!" and they both laughed at that.

Leanne pulled the plug from the sink and reached for the dishwashing detergent. Just this last load to get through then she could join the others in the next room and have another glass of white.

As the sink refilled, almost overflowing with foamy bubbles, Leanne's mother asked, "Did I ever tell you about the doll I got for Christmas when I was five?"

"No," Leanne replied, and then blinked. Honestly, her mother hadn't told her much at all about her childhood, and that realisation suddenly seemed strange.

"I called him Geoffrey. He had this sweet little blue woollen jumpsuit and his eyes closed when you lay him down."

"That's cute," Leanne replied vaguely as she scrubbed a particularly stubborn piece of burnt potato off the side of her Pyrex dish.

66

"Pushing Geoffrey around the backyard in his stroller is probably my only happy memory from my childhood."

Leanne paused. That couldn't be right, surely? She knew her mother was estranged from her own parents, which was why she barely knew her grandparents herself, but could things really have been so bad that her mother literally only had *one* happy memory?

Shocked and uncomfortable, ill-equipped to respond to this unfamiliar intimacy, Leanne's mind raced to find something else to talk about. Her own childhood had been full of pleasant memories, so she tried to steer the conversation in that direction.

"Do you remember how we all used to have our photos taken with Santa when we were kids?"

"Oh yes!" her mother replied, "But not just as kids! I seem to remember you getting yours taken right through into your teens. I think I still have all the photos somewhere."

"You should find them and put them out with the Christmas decorations," Leanne suggested.

"Oh, I don't know about that," her mother replied, "I never really liked those fake Santas."

"Who doesn't like *Santa*?" Leanne scoffed, but as she turned to her mother she saw her lips set tight in a straight line.

"They all had that same horrible laugh – 'Ho ho ho' – it reminded me of my father. I've always found something sinister about the laughter of men. You know how it is."

Leanne didn't, and she tried to square this with what little she could remember of her grandfather. He had never seemed 'sinister' to her, but she had only met him a handful of times when she was very young.

"That's why I married your father," Leanne's mother continued, snapping Leanne out of her reverie, "He never laughed."

This was an exaggeration, of course, but, Leanne had to admit, not by much.

"Of course, over time I found that he sneered. Especially at my stories."

Her hands buried deep in the greyish dishwater, Leanne struggled to take this in. How was she supposed to respond to this? Through the closed door she heard the muffled sounds of the rest of her family making merry and more than ever she wished she was out in the other room with her brothers drinking and laughing and not thinking about anything much in particular. She had to say something, though.

"I didn't know you wrote."

Leanne's mother snorted, "Not anymore!"

"What did you write?"

Leanne's mother waved off the question with a flap of the soggy tea towel, "Oh, just silly little things. Don't you remember the bedtime stories I told you when you were little?"

"Of course," replied Leanne, and she did. Vividly. Strange stories about children going on magical quests and encountering fantastic beings. Never for a moment had she considered that her mother had made up these stories herself, "I always thought you got them from a book."

Her mother laughed bitterly, "I used to want to be published. I was even working on a manuscript, but of course, that didn't go anywhere."

"Why not?" asked Leanne.

"Well, it was around that time that I had Alan," her mother replied. "When you have a child who you were just sort of melts away. You're re-cast as 'mother'. It's worth it, of course," and at this she reached over and squeezed Leanne's arm gently and oh, so briefly, "But you do sort of miss the bits of you that you leave behind."

Leanne drew one hand out of the sink and placed it lightly on the swell of her belly, leaving a damp patch on her cotton dress. She thought of the child that was growing inside of her and felt the stirring of a fear that had not been there before. She had wanted this child for so long, but she didn't want to lose herself. Not only this, but she didn't want to pass her mother's scars down to a new generation. After all, what if the baby was a girl? Worse yet, she thought with a surge of dread, what if it wasn't?

Suddenly Leanne was overcome with a feeling of fierce affection for her mother. It was more than just love, but a combination of this and a sense of empathy and, yes, pity too. Her chest inflated until the words, impossible to contain, slipped out of her, "I love you."

"I love you, too" came her mother's automatic response, and Leanne felt herself grow lighter, but only for a moment, as after a considered pause her mother continued, "...Sometimes I don't *like* you."

Leanne doubled over as if struck in the gut. She leaned in close to the sink. It was not very full (she hated to waste water) but there was still enough to drown in she thought as her nose grazed the dish foam. After all, it doesn't take much.

"Like when you're sulking," her mother clarified. Leanne, winded, could not muster a response.

"You're not sulking *now* are you?" her mother snapped her head to the side to glare at Leanne sternly. Somehow Leanne managed the straighten up and forced a laugh, "What? Sulking? What would I be sulking about?" Leanne repeated her hollow laugh then returned her gaze to the sink, a rictus grin frozen on her face as she scrubbed frantically at a crusty bit of pork baked-on to her roasting pan. She could feel her mother watching her critically, looking for a break in her facade, but Leanne kept smiling and, eventually, her mother returned her attention to drying the dishes.

Leanne tried again and again to swallow the lump in her throat. If she could just get through these last few dishes she could go off the bathroom and have a good cry. She had to hold out till then, though.

Just then, the door opened again and Auntie Cathy soared through with another load of dishes. "That's all that's left of them!" She was gone before Leanne, confused and disoriented even through her pain, could say anything.

Leanne looked at the pile of dirty dishes beside her, just as tall as it had been a moment... a few minutes... an hour ago.

She turned to her mother for answers, but the woman's eyes were as glassy as a doll's as she said, "Did I ever tell you about the doll I got for Christmas when I was just a child?"

TWELVE NIGHTS

KATHERINE KITCHENER

BONE-WHITE BOOMERS

THE SUN HUNG LOW in the hazy sky. Somewhere, not far away, the whole world was burning but here the fires were just streaks of watermelon pink in an orange sky and the pernicious miasma of smoke that infiltrated every square inch of air.

Coffee mug in hand, Simone stared out through the kitchen window and over the bare, dry paddock that stretched all the way to the levee bank. She took sips from her drink, too hot because she had forgone the milk, and surveyed the swirl of virulent colours on the far, but not far enough, horizon. They had their plan in place for if the fires came too close. They had already packed the ute in fact, but that didn't stop Simone running through a checklist in her head: clothes, toiletries, water, first-aid kit, passports and other important documents, phone charger, blankets, hard drives, wedding album. Snugs would have to come, too, but of course he could not be packed in advance. Simone looked over at the kitchen table where Liam was clutching the stuffed donkey tightly with one arm while he scribbled on a piece of paper with the other, a look of intense focus on the young child's face.

"What are you writing, honey?" Simone asked and Liam broke his concentration to smile up at his mother, "My list to Santa!" he said brightly.

Simone winced. She had almost forgotten that Christmas was right around the corner. She thought of the small pile of presents she and Julian had stashed away in their wardrobe and felt a pang. "Now, honey, you remember what we said? Santa may not be able to bring as many presents this year."

"But I've been really good!" insisted Liam, then he frowned and asked quietly, "Haven't I?"

Simone paused and that brief lapse left enough time for Liam's face to fall. His lip began to tremble.

"Oh, Liam, honey, of course you've been good!" Simone rushed to her son's side, covering the top of his head with a flurry of kisses. For a moment she considered just dropping the whole facade about Christmas, Santa and everything. "It's just that..." Liam looked up at her and his eyes were wide and bright. He's still so young, thought Simone. Too young. She took a deep breath, "It's just that some years Santa just doesn't make as many toys."

Liam ran the back of his hand over his eyes a few times and Simone was relieved to see that no tears came. "Now if you're done with that list why don't you and Snugs go play in your room." Liam slid off his chair and, squeezing Snugs tighter still, ambled off in the direction of his bedroom.

With a sigh, Simone picked up her coffee again and took a fortifying sip before reaching for the piece of paper her son has left on the table. She scanned the list and could not help but smile. After all that, it was quite modest, really. Simone's relief was mingled with pride at the thought of her son's lack of materialism. He was certainly no spoiled brat. Simone's mind turned toward something she read once about there being only two possible solutions to the problem of not having everything you want, either acquire more; or want less.

People were going to have to learn to want less these days, Simone mused. Lots of people were doing it rough this year. There were always fires, of course, but this year was worse. The dry season had started earlier than usual and there was no sign of relief. Her family had made their plan for if the fires came too close (essentially, run). Simone liked to have plans in place, but this one offered her little comfort. There was so much they'd have to leave behind and risk losing forever – a family home, the mementos her mother had handed down to her, a whole lifetime's worth of accumulated stuff.

The risk of fire meant there would be no fireworks this new year either, but Simone scolded herself for getting ahead of things. They had to make it through Christmas, first. Simone looked out again at the glowing sky. It really was beautiful, though.

*

Walking past Liam's bedroom as she headed off to bed, Simone heard a shuffling from within. She frowned. It has been almost two hours since her son's bedtime and he is usually such a sound sleeper. Slowly she opened the door and peeked inside.

Liam was sitting bolt upright in bed, the doona clenched tightly in both hands. When he saw Simone at the door he whispered excitedly, "Did you hear it, too?"

"Hear what?" asked Simone, stepping into the room and closing the door behind her to block out the glow of the loungeroom lights. She stepped up to Liam's bed and began to smooth the bedclothes around him.

TWELVE NIGHTS

"The reindeer!" hissed Liam, "On the roof!" Simone hid her smile. "It's a little too early for reindeer, sweetie," she explained, "It was probably just a possum." Simone guided her sleepy son back to his pillow, and he lay down without argument, sleep already beginning to settle on his soft features. "I know it was a reindeer," he insisted with a yawn, then closed his eyes. "Okay, honey," Simone replied quietly as she leaned in to kiss Liam on the forehead, "Goodnight, now."

Later that night, as she lay tired but sleepless in her bed, Julian softly snoring beside her, Simone heard something on the roof. She frowned. It doesn't sound like a possum. There was no scratching or scuttling, no hiss, just a low, regular thump. Simone could not work out what the sound was, but her exhausted mind couldn't seem to be too bothered by it, either. The rhythm matched her heartbeat and gradually sent her to sleep.

*

The next day Simone was a whirlwind of activity – dusting, vacuuming, sweeping. She got through a week's worth of chores in a few short hours, largely because she has no other distractions. Rather than playing in the garden, watching TV or just otherwise hovering about his mother, Liam had spent the whole morning shut up in his room. Once or twice Simone had gone to check on him, but each time she stopped herself at the door. She could hear her son in there playing quietly and decided to go off and fit some more cleaning in rather than risk disturbing her boy in his uncharacteristically independent activity.

While Simone was halfway through mopping the kitchen floor, she saw Liam's door slowly creep open. Without ceasing her own activity, she watched out of the corner of her eye as Liam emerged carrying the plastic crate that he kept his soft toys in. What had become of the soft toys themselves, Simone could only guess. Scattered all over his bedroom floor, most likely. Liam carried the empty crate towards the kitchen door, his face set in a look of determination so far beyond his years that Simone had to hide a smile.

"Going to play outside, honey?" Simone asked brightly, as Liam carefully placed the crate on the floor and reached for the handle of the sliding door. "Yep." He replied without so much as turning to glance at his mother. He pushed the crate outside then followed it, closing the door behind himself. Simone paused her mopping briefly to watch Liam as he carried the crate to the edge of the verandah then disappeared with it down the side of the house. Simone smiled. Perhaps the crate would be a sailing ship or a rocket or a train. The boundless creativity of children always buoyed her heart.

Once all her chores were done Simone took a moment to survey the results of her labour with satisfaction. Their home may not be the biggest, but it was clean and orderly, or as much so as was possible with a toddler in the household. Thinking of her son, Simone peeked into his bedroom to see what sort of state it was in. The soft toys were, indeed, left lying on the floor, but they were mostly in a neat pile in the centre of the room.

As it was almost time for lunch, Simone decided to bring Liam in from outside. She went out the back and around the side of the house where she had seen her son go. There was no Liam and no crate, but there was a mark in the dusty earth running from the garden tap all the way around the corner to the front of the house. Frowning, Simone followed the tracks and found Liam in the middle of the front yard, slowly dragging the crate which was now clearly full of water.

Simone took a deep breath and silently counted to three. "What on earth are you up to, Liam?" she sighed. Liam looked up and grinned "It's for the reindeer! In case they're thirsty." Simone took in another slow, deep breath. The crate was a big one, and Liam had filled it almost to the brim. She was surprised he had managed to drag it that far at all and supposed he must have just been *that* determined.

She thought about scolding him for wasting water, but as she looked into his eyes, bright with excitement, she sighed in resignation instead. It would give the magpies something to drink, at least. The poor, thirsty things had been hanging about the yard, their beaks hanging open plaintively. Simone reached out a hand to her son, "Let's go and have some lunch."

*

Simone lay awake in bed, as was becoming her habit. Even on her good days, on the days where she had accomplished much, had spent some time outdoors and had pleasant interactions with people she cared about, by the time night fell her mind was abuzz and she was unable to shut it off. Sometimes she worried about money or work. Sometimes she worried about Liam. Often, she worried about nothing in particular but just felt a kind of existential dread weighing down on her chest until it felt like she might sink through the bed, the floor, the earth... All the way through to its molten core.

She kept her eyes closed and tried to focus on her breathing, the sensation of the bed sheet against her skin. Anything other than the miasmic machinations of her consciousness. She squeezed her eyes tight and listened to the thud, thud, thud of her heart – counting each beat. She made it to twenty before noticing the other sound undercutting it. It was the same pounding sound she had heard the night before. It was not just coming from the roof this time, but seemed to be all around the house converging on the front yard. Again, she couldn't place it. All her mind was able to conjure up was a large group of people all marching out of unison with each other

That couldn't be right, she knew, but the idea of a band of trespassers or intruders stuck with her even after the sound came to a gradual halt petering out from a multitude of thumps to a few straggling taps.

Her eyes open now, Simone lay rigid in bed. She thought of waking Julian, slumbering peacefully beside her, but the thought of his possible derision at her anxiety seemed worse than whatever the source itself may actually be. Eventually, she slipped out of the bed, put on her slippers and headed for the front door.

Outside, away from the air-conditioning, the night was oppressively hot. To stop the heat invading the house, Simone closed the door conscientiously behind herself as she stood on the front porch peering out into the front yard. It was empty, or seemed to be at least. It was hard to tell because the haze from the fires was thicker than usual and Simone couldn't see through it. She squinted, her eyes already starting to burn, and continued to try and look through the haze. Then, out of the swirling smoke, a figure emerged – hunched and long-eared with a thick, muscular tail and eyes that burnt like embers. A kangaroo.

Simone was so relieved she nearly laughed. Certainly, there was no danger here, and she was glad she had not woken her husband. It was unusual to see a roo this close to the house, though. Usually, they preferred the flat, grassy expanse of the golf course on the edge of town.

Something was still not right. Simone tried to see through the dark and the swirling white smoke until she finally realised the problem – the kangaroo was *made* of smoke. The edges of the animal were soft and amorphous and gave off a spectral glow. As the white smoke curled and parted, Simone caught a glimpse of even whiter bone peeking out from charred flesh.

There were others, she soon realised. Half a dozen of the eerie things in total, all assembling around the plastic toy tub. One leaned down and stuck out a misty tongue. It did not so much as disturb the surface of the water. This did not seem to deter it, though, and the spectre continued to lap. Simone wondered if the poor thing was getting any relief for its efforts or if it was something like Tantalus forever reaching for the water in vain. The other roos all leaned in and took their turn.

*

Despite Simone's lack of sleep, it was Julian who was grumpy at breakfast the next morning. He munched his cereal without comment and Simone and Liam both knew from his silence and the look on his face to leave him be.

Julian dumped his empty bowl in the kitchen sink and then scowled out the front window, "What is that bucket of water there for, anyway?" he grumbled. His family knew that he did not really want an answer; that he barely even registered them as present.

"It's going to attract mozzies. I'll go and empty it on the back garden."

Simone and Liam cried, "No!" in unison and the sound was enough to make Julian's attention snap back to the kitchen. He frowned quizzically at his wife.

"Leave it, honey," Simone simpered, then cast a glance at Liam as she said, "It's for the reindeer."

TWELVE NIGHTS

THE SCENT OF PINE

ALEX OPENED THE FIRST BOX gingerly, as if he expected its contents to leap out at him, and in a way they did. Once free of their cardboard prison the plastic branches sprung up, almost knocking his glasses off.

Meaghan emerged from the kitchen bearing drinks, only to find her partner grimacing at the boxes in distaste.

"Why are there, two boxes?" grumbled Alex.

Meaghan shrugged as she set the ice water down on the coffee table, "I told you it was a big tree."

"No," Alex corrected. "What you said was 'It'll fit.'"

"And it will," Meaghan insisted, "It's not that big!"

Alex huffed and crossed his arms in front of his chest, "I dunno. It feels wrong. It's not really Christmas without a real tree. It just doesn't feel the same. It doesn't *smell* the same."

"This is a real tree," Meaghan insisted. "My family has had it for as long as I can remember. Anyway, we've been over this. I don't want to be sweeping up pine needles every five minutes and I don't want to risk the kittens eating them. You know it can perforate their bowels!" As if on cue, Noodle yowled in displeasure, whereas Trixie merely yawned and stretched. Alex continued to glare silently at the boxes. "Grandma used to spray it with air freshener," Meaghan offered weakly.

Meaghan stepped towards Alex and dragged the first layer of the plastic tree out of the box. Alex, relenting, felt about in the box for the base and eventually retrieved a metal cross from somewhere among the wire and plastic branches.

The first layer of the tree was low and wide and even bigger than Meaghan remembered, "I told you it was big!" she crowed. Setting that first layer firmly in the base, the couple began spreading out the branches. It was looking thicker and fuller than Alex expected. Maybe even more so than a real pine tree, though of course he would not say this aloud.

Luckily for them, the tree seemed to have been put away in order. Meaghan was not surprised, "Grandma always did like to keep things neat and tidy. 'A place for everything and everything in its place', that kind of thing." The second layer slid smoothly on top of the first. "I remember one time Poppa came home and didn't take his boots off at the front door. Nana chased him all around the front yard with a willow switch!"

"Oh, so she wasn't philosophically opposed to real trees, then?" Alex asked archly, but Meaghan only scoffed.

The third layer was barely any smaller than the first two. "It's not going to fit," announced Alex, even as they heaved that layer on top of the others.

"Yeah, it will," insisted Meghan, but Alex could hear the uncertainty in her voice. Alex and Meaghan stepped back to survey the monstrous proportions of the tree so far, its branches already blocking out most of their TV. "Still think it will fit?" Alex asked. Meaghan set her lips. "We can watch TV on the laptop," she declared, then stalked back over to the boxes and started on the next layer. Alex sighed as he followed.

Spreading out the branches of the fourth layer Meaghan began dreamily, "When I was really little I used to hide among the branches. I'd crawl between them right to the centre of the tree and imagine I was in Narnia. It was like my own little world. Once I hid in there and listened to my mum looking for me for half an hour!"

"I'll bet your mum was pretty pissed off when she found you," Alex observed.

Meaghan frowned, "Actually, she seemed more scared than angry. I suppose she thought I'd run off somewhere. I wasn't allowed to play with the tree after that – only look. Mum said she was worried about me breaking Grandma's ornaments, but I think she just didn't want to lose me again."

"Where are your grandmother's ornaments?" asked Alex as he heaved the fifth layer up onto the stack, "Did Chloe get them?"

"I don't think so," Meaghan replied uncertainly, "I'm not really sure what happened to them. I don't remember seeing them when we were sorting through Grandma's stuff."

Alex took a step back and placed his hands on his hips, surveying the vast bulk of what was the tree so far. "We'll have to buy more ornaments," he concluded after finishing his appraisal, "It's going to look too bare otherwise."

Alex waited but Meaghan did not reply. The only response he received was a slight, cool draught that faintly stirred the plastic needles of the tree. Alex closed his eyes and took a moment to appreciate the relief from the summer heat.

There were just two more layers left to go, and for that Alex was relieved. Although the layers got slightly smaller the further up the tree they went, he still wouldn't call any of them 'small', and the effort it took to hoist each one higher and higher up the trunk was more than he had accounted for. Once the sixth layer was in position Alex sighed heavily and took a swig of his drink. The ice had already melted.

"How long did you say your family has had this tree?" Alex asked, noting again the fullness of the branches, the perfect condition of each individual needle.

"Oh, a long time." Meaghan replied from somewhere behind the tree, "Generations."

"Huh," was all Alex could think to say. Surely plastic Christmas trees hadn't been around for all that long? And when had Meaghan's family come to Australia, anyway? Would anyone really bring a Christmas tree with them when immigrating? He kept his quibbles to himself, though. After all, what did he know about fake Christmas trees? His family always had real ones.

They were at the final layer now, anyway. Alex had to stand on the coffee table to reach high enough to get the top in position and, when he did, he found that the very tip of the tree scraped the ceiling so that it bent down slightly.

"There!" Meaghan cried triumphantly, "It fits!"

Alex scoffed "There's no room for a star!"

"Angel." Meaghan's voice came to him softly, "Grandma always had an angel." Her voice seemed faint and far away.

Alex climbed down from the table and took a couple of steps back, bumping into the sofa. The tree was huge. It took up the entire room. He couldn't even see Meaghan anymore. "How did it even fit in those boxes?" he wondered.

Another gust, no longer refreshing but icy, stirred the plastic branches. Alex shivered.

Just then, Alex heard one of the kittens rustling in the branches. Suddenly he was incensed. The one reason he had agreed to this tree, this towering eyesore, was that he thought the kittens would leave it alone. He couldn't see which kitten it was, but of course it was Noodle. Alex parted the branches but they seemed impossibly thick. Impossibly deep. Once again he saw movement in the branches and this time heard the accompanying jingle of a bell. Alex twisted himself sideways and pushed deeper into the branches.

No longer did the tree smell of the lingering ghost of cheap air freshener. Here in the branches it smelled like a forest. Alex heard the bell again and kept going deeper. Where was Noodle? Where was the trunk of the tree, for that matter? As he progressed it seemed to get colder and colder. He heard the bell again.

This time, Alex stopped as he remembered something. The kittens had been inside all day. Alex and Meaghan had not wanted to take them out in the heat. They were not wearing their collars.

Alex turned to go back. He struggled to push his way out from the branches and in his haste tripped on a tree root and landed on his hands and knees in snow. He heard the jingling once more from somewhere above. Now the sound was closer he could hear that it was not just one bell but many. Like sleigh bells. Or, at least, like sleigh bells sounded in movies. A shadow fell across the snow as something heavy landed in the tree's branches.

He was not really sure what he was looking at. It was something like an owl but vast and disproportionate, its breast a broad and snowy expanse flecked with tawny brown. From its left side sprouted four great wings, and from its right another three as well as a bloody stump where an eighth may once have been. Each wing was festooned with rows of silver bells that jingled in the icy wind. Its horned feet were red and dripping with unnamed viscera. It blinked its seven great black eyes (not brown, but truly black) at Alex and he saw behind them – nothing at all. No malice, but no kindness either. No thought at all, really. All he saw when he looked at the creature was himself reflected back as seven perfect miniatures. He saw himself for the tiny, insignificant thing he was. Little more than a mote in the mighty creature's eye.

As he lay cowering in the snow, Alex thought he heard Meaghan's voice coming from somewhere far away. Faint, sweet and without a hint of irony. "See, it's not that big."

EVIL SANTA

WORKING IN A SECOND-HAND BOOKSTORE had always seemed like the ideal job to Anthony. He loved books, after all. After three years working at Past Tense Books, however, Anthony learned that he did not love books half as much as he hated customers.

The shop's owner, Tristan, was as eccentric as Anthony had always expected a used book dealer to be, but in an affected and ostentatious way that set Anthony's teeth on edge. Worse yet, Tristan seemed to make a practice of hiring anyone who asked for a job, so Anthony worked with a revolving door of casuals and part-timers, all of them with varying degrees of literary knowledge and retail experience and each of them, in their own unique ways, just the worst.

So how could he be expected to choose a gift for people he didn't know or like? Anthony brooded on this while wandering the overcrowded shopping centre that was mercifully within walking distance of his apartment (parking was impossible at this time of year, or so he had been reliably informed). They were doing a KK thing at the work Christmas party tomorrow and Anthony still hadn't bought his present.

Tristan wanted to do something different (of course) so apparently they would all be playing "Evil Santa" for their Kris Kringle. Instead of drawing names and buying a gift for a specific person, all the gifts would be pooled and then there would be some sort of game to see who got which present... Anthony hadn't really been paying attention when Tristan explained his plan.

Hurried and harried and jostled for the last time, Anthony made a snap decision and an about turn to head for the cinema. Surely no one could complain about movie vouchers as a Christmas present. Although, he admitted to himself grimly as the ticket clerk slid over the vouchers, if anyone in the world was likely to complain it *would* be his co-workers.

*

The shopfront window of Past Tense Books was tastefully decorated with a few strands of white fairy lights and a restrained display of Victorian ghost stories and the obligatory Dickens. Christmassy, but not too Christmassy. Anthony had been the one to set it up and he gave it an appreciative, almost proprietorial glance on his way into the party.

Unlike in previous years, Tristan had decided to host the staff Christmas party in the shop rather than at the local pub. Money was tight this year, Anthony had seen just enough of the accounts to know that. It made little difference to him, though. He never stayed for the entire party, just long enough to fulfill the obligation.

As Anthony entered he saw the gifts sitting by the checkout and slipped the envelope with the movie tickets into the pile before looking for a drink.

Although Anthony knew Tristan to keep a fine bottle of peaty whiskey under his desk, he knew not to expect any such luxuries at the party. In fact, the only refreshment there seemed to be of the liquid variety was a large bowl of fruit punch. Anthony scooped himself a cup and sipped it tentatively. The concoction was cloyingly sweet, although the mint leaves gave it a strangely bitter aftertaste. At least it was alcoholic.

Anthony had barely had a second sip of his punch when Leanne, already several drinks in zeroed in on him and he spent the next twenty minutes being gradually close-talked into a corner. He was almost relieved when Tristan called them all together for the gift exchange.

The group congregated in the small open space in front of the counter, forming a tight circle wedged between the discount crate (crammed full of E. L. James paperbacks and other well-worn "romance" novels). As Tristan stepped into the circle he did not look like a man whose business was teetering on the edge of collapse. He had his habitual, knowing smirk and was wearing his usual tweed jacket and horn-rimmed glasses and—

—Anthony blinked. Was Tristan *actually* wearing a Tudor bonnet? His boss *was* a Doctor of Philosophy, something that anyone who had spoken to him for five minutes knew, but surely no one actually wore those things after the graduation ceremony.

As if reading Anthony's mind, Tristan swept the bonnet off his head dramatically. "Sit down, sit down, boys and girls!" the thirty-something-year-old man proclaimed, "It is now time for all good children to get what they deserve."

After the briefest of pauses, but without comment, the shop workers all settled themselves on the floor like school children while Tristan began stacking the KK presents in a pile at the centre of the circle. As he bustled about between counter and floor Tristan explained, "The rules of *Evil Santa* are elegant in their simplicity. Everyone takes turns. In your turn, you choose a gift from the middle. You can then choose whether to unwrap the gift for yourself or force a trade with someone who has already unwrapped one. Understand?"

Although Anthony understood well enough, the whole thing sounded to him more 'needlessly convoluted' than 'elegantly simple.' Still he forced a smile and nodded with the others, trying to calculate in his mind how long this whole pantomime would last and whether he'd be home in time to enjoy a quiet dram before bed.

"But how do we decide what order we go in?" asked Nathan, the shop's dedicated accountant and business adviser, and the only full-timer other than Anthony. In response, Tristan tapped at the side of his nose with a manicured index finger, then pulled his bonnet out from behind his back and jiggled it playfully. He then reached into the velvety cap and pulled out a slip of paper with a flourish. He peered at the slip. "James," he announced.

The newest of the store's endless stream of recruits jumped at the sound of his name, then lurched forward, scrambling as he untangled his crossed legs. With a moment's hesitation, James selected the largest present in the pile, then returned to his place in the circle. Everyone, even Anthony, leaned in to watch as the gawky teenager tore layer after layer of coloured paper off his prize to reveal... a jumbo pack of toilet paper.

"Oooh, triple-ply," cooed Carol (the on-and-off weekend casual) mockingly, "Fancy!" James flushed crimson.

As the next gift – a depressed garden gnome – was unwrapped, Anthony wondered if he, too, should have bought a gag gift.

The third name out f the hat was Leanne. She selected a gold-wrapped cylinder and settled back in her spot. She examined the wrapped gift but rather than opening it looked back to the middle of the circle, then turned quizzically to Tristan, "Why are there eight presents when there's only seven of us?"

Everyone turned to the middle and counted. Sure enough, including the two presents already opened and the one in Leanne's hands there were eight in total.

"Did someone buy two presents?" Nathan asked. Everyone looked about expectantly, but no one spoke up.

"Now, now," chided Tristan, spinning around on his heels to address the small gathering as though he were the ringmaster of a circus. "We can't ask people to divulge what they bought. That's not in the spirit of the game!"

Ultimately, Leanne decided to trade her still-wrapped gift for the toilet paper, "You can never have too much!" she chirpped. James unwrapped the golden gift and revealed it to be a huge tub of liquorice all-sorts.

"Perhaps with was supposed to go *with* the toilet paper," he said glumly.

As the game progressed things got tense. Everyone wanted to trade and no one was happy about the outcome when they did. Arguments broke out about who bought which presents and what they *meant* in choosing a particular gift, every generic gift somehow becoming an imagined personal slight.

Finally, Anthony's name was drawn from the hat. "Lucky last!" beamed Tristan. Anthony crawled to the centre of the circle. All that was left was the envelope with the movie tickets he purchased and one other gift. Anthony reached for the envelope but then hesitated. There was nothing particularly interesting out at the cinema at the moment. Did he really want to sit in the dark with strangers and watch some mediocre flick he would probably forget just days after seeing? Besides, if he chose the tickets the other present would be left over and he would probably never find out what it was, or whose feelings may be hurt by it. Anthony's hand wavered, and then at the last moment he snatched the other present and tore off the paper.

It was a book. *How original*, thought Anthony. It was, in fact, a slim, Moleskine notebook. Anthony was mildly pleased. This was something he could use at least. As he flicked through the pages, however, he found that they were already filled with cramped, barely-legible handwriting. Anthony wished he had chosen the tickets, but as he looked up he found the envelope had already been whisked away somewhere, presumably by Tristan, and the group, still sniping and bickering, had gotten up off the floor and started to disperse.

Tristan turned the music back up and Anthony retreated to a nook near the refreshments table. He opened the book and tried to decipher the scribbled text.

Leanne found him again and started talking, but Anthony did not look up. He continued to peer at the book as his co-worker nattered on when suddenly the word 'Leanne' seemed to leap off the page at him. Anthony squinted at the name until he could make out the words around it, 'Leanne got Gary fired.'

Anthony remembered Gary. He had seemed like a quiet, unassuming young man at first, but he left the shop under something of a cloud. His interest piqued, Anthony stared at the cramped, spidery writing until he was finally able to make some sense out of it. He read on.

It was an interesting read. A sordid little tale about how Leanne, apparently spurned by Gary, forged a plot to ruin him. According to the notebook, Leanne had seeded rumours about Gary, letting the general sentiment against him among the other employees fester before finally making complaints to Tristan. Reading the details, Anthony frowned, realising that Leanne had said some of these things to him. Had he believed her at the time? Maybe. He hadn't particularly cared either way, but he certainly didn't speak up for Gary when the whispers spread.

Looking up from the book, Anthony met Leanne's eyes directly and asked, "How's Gary? Do you still see much of him?"

At this, Leanne purpled, then turned on her heels and stalked off, her uncharacteristic silence gratifying.

Anthony smirked, snapping the notebook shut and tapping it to his chin. Perhaps this gift would be useful after all. He drained his drink and went to get a refill. While taking a hearty gulp of the bitter-sweet punch Anthony tried to see what else was written in the book. It was still mostly indecipherable and Anthony was about to give up in frustration when he finally saw the words, "Nathan cooks the books".

At the other side of the room, Nathan was leaning in attentively as Tristan talked (mostly with his hands). Anthony took another swig of his drink and swaggered over.

"Nathan!" Anthony cried cordially as he approached, reaching out a free hand to clasp the accountant's arm. Startled, Nathan looked up.

"I've been meaning to tell you how great your new watch looks!" Anthony beamed.

Nathan looked down at his other wrist. "Thanks," he muttered and made to turn back towards Tristan before Anthony continued, "Cartier, is it?"

"Yes," Nathan replied warily.

Anthony let out a low whistle. "Nice! That must have set you back a bit. I'd hate to think how long you'd have to save for a watch like that." Nathan shifted uncomfortably while Tristan frowned in the background.

"Well, I'll leave you two to enjoy yourselves," Anthony said while giving Nathan a hearty pat on the back. He turned to Tristan and said with a wink, 'You'd better *watch* out for this one!"

Walking back towards the refreshment table Anthony was elated. He felt powerful. For the first time in his professional life, he felt like he had the upper hand. His head swimming with drink and glee, Anthony flicked back and forth through the notebook to see what other gems he could find.

The letters seemed to crawl across the page and tangle up with one another. Anthony frowned. Had he really had that much to drink?

As he stared intently at the writhing text Anthony was vaguely aware of someone coughing somewhere behind him and then a loud thud as something heavy fell to the floor.

Anthony's stomach suddenly started to cramp so violently that he dropped his half-finished drink to clutch at his mid-section. He kept a grip on the notebook, though. Even through the pain, he could not bear to turn his attention away. Finally, though his vision was swimming, Anthony made out one last phrase written in the book.

"Tristan poisoned the punch."

TWELVE NIGHTS

CARD ONLY

JUDITH FLICKED THROUGH THE MAIL. Bill, bill, bill. She frowned. Hadn't they just paid off that one? She sighed and tossed it aside with the others. She sat back in her chair and took a sip of tea, gazing over at the row of cards on her mother's old display cabinet. It was already December 19 and they had received only eight Christmas cards so far. Not that Judith had sent out that many, herself, but still. There used to be so many more.

Glancing once more at the pile of mail in front of her, Judith noticed one marked with a "Card Only" sticker. She smiled and set down the tea, reaching for the envelope and opening it hungrily. The card inside depicted a winter scene with a snow-covered cottage and a red-breasted robin. Judith felt a pang as she remembers her mother, who always loved birds. She took a deep breath and let the bitter-sweet nostalgia wash over her for a while.

It was actually getting harder and harder to find Christmas cards like this these days. The seasonal disparity must put a lot of people off. Still, even though Judith had only ever known summer Christmases, this snowy scene and cheerful robin still somehow reminded her of what Christmas was like when she was a child. She felt a swelling in her own breast and realised that there is a part of that old magic that never really fades.

She was still looking at the front of the card when Warren stepped in from the garden. He looked over Judith's shoulder and remarked, "Gee, that's a nice card!"

"Isn't it?" Judith agreed.

"Who's it from?"

"Oh!" Judith cried, realising she hasn't even opened the card yet. She opened it and then frowned. It was completely blank. She closed the card to examine the front again, then flicked it over to look at the back. Nothing. She laughed. Someone was obviously in such a hurry getting their Christmas cards done they had slipped an empty one in my accident. But who? Judith grabbed for the envelope and checks it but there is no return address. She examined the front of the envelope, noticing for the first time that the address was not handwritten, but typed. As in, with a *typewriter*. Judith strained to think who she knew who even owned a typewriter, let alone used it.

It was then that she noticed the stamp has been postmarked. Another anachronism, she thought. It seems that these days Australia Post only postmarked stamps if you went into the post office and specifically asked them to. She squinted at the blurry ink, trying to make out the location. Eventually, she was able to make out the postcode: 3844. Traralgon.

"So it's from Anne!" Judith thought triumphantly. This really wasn't a surprise. Her sister always sent out Christmas cards and she had a love of vintage objects – cameras, old rotary telephones, vintage vinyl. Of course *she* would have a typewriter!

With a small chuckle, Judith stood and began to clear the table for dinner. She gathered up the blank card with the rest of the junk mail and empty envelopes and was about to toss it in the recycling with the rest, but hesitated. It really was a pretty card. It would be a shame to just throw it out, and when she has received so few others, after all. Judith picked the card out of the pile and, discarding the other waste without looking, went and put it on the display cabinet with the others.

That evening, Warren's daughter visited and it was lovely. It was always lovely, but somehow that night Judith was awash with melancholy. She thought of all the family she had lost over the years. Her mother, of course, but all the other extended relatives that she never knew, or barely knew. She didn't have a big family like lots of people. Like Warren. Sometimes she felt completely cut off from the rest of the world.

This was the first time Judith and Warren had seen Natalie since the wedding, so of course there was much talk of the special day and what a success it was. Judith smiled and nodded and graciously accepted Natalie's thank-you card, which was handmade and featured a photo of Judith and Warren at the reception. "What a lovely photo!" Judith gushed, and it really was, except...

In the background, somewhere behind Judith's right shoulder, was a man she did not recognise. This was not surprising in itself – Judith really only knew a handful of Natalie's family and friends, and virtually none of Ben's – but there was something off about this man. His suit was ill-fitting and his scarlet waistcoat looked a little too old-fashioned for someone not even in the bridal party. More notable, though, was the awkward way his head was tilted to the side, as if he was listening to something or, more accurately, performing a pantomime of someone listening to something. Judith said nothing but, as Natalie took them through the rest of the photos she has brought with her, Judith kept noticing the man pop up again and again. Always in the background and always with the oddly wry neck. Judith tried to ignore the man, feeling guilty for noticing his odd appearance and for being made uncomfortable by it.

When Natalie left Judith placed the thank you card on the dresser. It may not be a Christmas card, as such, but it served nicely to pad out the ranks of the others.

That night Judith dreamt of her mother, but not *as* her mother. She dreamt that her mother was a child, as Judith has only seen her in a few faded sepia photographs. The dream was in colour, though, or partly anyway. A red sun rose over red rooftops and the little girl that was her mother stood on the street in a red dress. A red robin landed next to her, but it was monstrously large. It pecked at the girl's neck and a trickle of red blood ran down, but she did not cry. In fact, her red lips parted in a beatific smile. The robin started to sing in a deep voice, but Judith did not catch the words before waking up.

It was 5 o'clock and Warren was already up and off to work. Judith did not have to be at her own job until that afternoon, so she pottered about in her dressing gown for a while, at something of a loose end. As she sat in the loungeroom with a cup of tea, her eyes were drawn to the robin card. After her dream, the picture did not seem so jolly now. The more she woke up, however, the less Judith remembered of her dream. By the time she had washed the breakfast dishes all that remained of the dream was a faint uneasiness and the bitter-sweet memory of her mother.

Thinking of her mother, Judith decided to pull out a box of her mother's old things that she had stored in the shed. The particular box she found, one of many, was full of all sorts of odds and ends and Judith picked through it listlessly, unable to find the comfort she sought. She found a slim, blue address book and flicked through it, noticing sadly that most of the pages were blank. She stopped when she eventually came across an entry. *Uncle Joseph.* Judith did not know the specific person, but the name was unsurprising. What person of Maltese descent could say they *didn't* have an Uncle Joe?

Something about the name worried at the loose threads of her memory until it eventually snagged on something and she remembered, as she had not done in years, the way her mother would threaten her when she misbehaved as a child: "If you don't behave I'll send you off to live with Uncle Joe."

The accompanying address, Judith realised, was in her hometown. So why didn't she know him? Had she just forgotten?

Flicking back and forth between the mostly-empty pages of the address book, Judith once again felt overcome with loneliness. Perhaps, if she really did have an Uncle Joe, now was the time to reach out?

Judith dug about in her handbag and pulled out a pen, tapping it against her lower lip thoughtfully before suddenly jumping up and grabbing the blank Christmas card off the display cabinet. Surely Anne wouldn't mind her reusing her card. Maybe it would even be a nice touch, as though the card had come from both of them.

Dear Uncle Joe,
I am sorry that I have never reached out before now. Since Mum (Kitty) passed away I have lost touch with most of her family, which I really think is a shame. It would be lovely if we could catch up in person sometime. You're always welcome in our home.
Wishing you a happy Christmas,
Judith Seychell.

Satisfied with her missive, Judith found a blank envelope and carefully copied out the address from the little blue book. She applied one of the cheaper Christmas stamps, being sure to mark the envelope "card only" and tucked it into her bag to post when she went into work.

Work was so busy that afternoon that Judith almost forgot about the card. It was only when changing cars at the end of the day that, fishing through her handbag for her keys, she came across the envelope. Luckily, the post office was not far from her parking spot, so she was able to quickly slip her card in the red postbox before returning to her car to head home.

That night as she was brushing her teeth, Judith's mother's voice echoed in her head "If you don't brush your teeth they'll end up brown and crooked like Uncle Joe's!" She spat, then laughed. Her mother really wasn't one to mince words when it came to other people's appearance.

Judith was tired that night, but decided to take a sleeping tablet anyway. She didn't have work the next day so it didn't matter if she was a bit groggy and she could really do with a decent night's rest. As she lay in bed waiting for the pill to take effect Judith let her mind wander, not focusing on any one thought in particular. As she began to feel drowsy a phrase drifted across her consciousness, unmistakably in her mother's voice "If you don't go to bed, Uncle Joe will come and sing the goodnight song." Judith frowned into her pillow. Had her mother actually said that, or was the sleeping pill scrambling her thoughts? Before she could interrogate the thought further, Judith sunk into a dreamless sleep.

The next day, Judith called her sister, just to check-in. "I found Uncle Joseph's address in mum's address book so I sent him off a card. You never mentioned he was living there in Traralgon."

There was silence on the line before Anne finally answered, a little cautiously it seemed to Judith, "Uncle Joseph doesn't live in Traralgon."

"Oh!" Judith said, "... Well, I was a little surprised when I saw the address. I thought all of Mum's family were still in Malta."

"Uncle Joseph doesn't live in Malta, either," Anne replied, "Well, not anymore."

Judith's heart sank. "I'm sorry?"

Anne heaved a sigh before proceeding, "It was a bit of a sore point of Mum's actually. Joseph was her mother's brother. He died when Mum was just a kid. I don't know the details, but it was bad enough or sordid enough that Mum's parents thought she was too fragile to know about it..."

Judith considered with wonder the idea of anyone considering her mother to be 'fragile'. Anne continued, "... So they never told her! They just said he'd moved away. It was only years later – well after our grandparents had passed away and Mum had moved to Australia – that she found out. A cousin mentioned it briefly in passing and Mum was devastated. Not so much at the loss of Joe – it had been so long since she'd seen him – but the fact that no one in her family had bothered to tell her, even well into her adulthood."

Judith was at a loss for words, but finally managed, "But whose address was it?"

Anne laughed "Just about every Maltese man in the Latrobe Valley is called 'Joseph'... and that's even assuming he is Maltese. It could be anyone."

"Oh drat!" cried Judith, "And I sent off that lovely card you gave me, too."

"Card?"

"The one with the robin."

"We haven't sent out Christmas cards, yet. It's been too busy. Speaking of, I'd really better head off now, Sis. Enjoy the holidays! We'll talk soon."

Judith absently murmured her goodbyes and hung up with a frown. She was now left with two mysteries: who was the "Uncle Joe" in her mother's address book and who had sent her the robin card to begin with?

*

The weeks leading up to Christmas passed quickly, without much to distinguish one day from another. Work. Home. Sleep. Repeat. If Judith was a little bored, at least she was comfortable. That was, until she received another envelope marked "card only".

Her address was typed on this envelope, just like the first, and Judith felt a knot of apprehension in her chest as she flicked to the back and saw there was no sender name or return address. Once she brought the envelope inside Judith sat for some time before she finally decided to open it.

Inside was not a card at all, but a photograph. An old one, too. It pictured a tall man and a little girl clutching a doll in a gingham dress. Judith recognised the doll, first. "Ginghy," she whispered, then looked up to see the miniature baby doll sitting in her display cabinet. So that made the girl...

... Yes, of course it was her mother. Judith could see it, now – the thick, wavy hair, the large, dark eyes. But who was this man beside her? He didn't look like Judith's grandfather. He was too old, to start with, and bore no familial resemblance however hard she squinted. What Judith noticed most about him, however, what really made her catch her breath, was the way his head was tilted too far to one side. Judith flipped the card over to look for an inscription, and found a note in the same typeface as the front of the envelope:

Thank you for the warm welcome. I'll be seeing you soon.
- Uncle Joe

*

Warren's kids were all planning to spend Christmas with their mother this year, so the weekend beforehand Judith and Warren were meeting them all at Natalie's place for some gift swapping and pre-Christmas cheer. As they headed off, Judith slipped the thank you card from Natalie's wedding into her purse.

The atmosphere at Natalie's house was, as was to be expected, even more convivial than usual. There was much chatter and laughter and mountains of food and if Judith was a little more withdrawn than usual, no one seemed to notice. The entire evening she held her purse firmly on her lap, as if she expected it to be snatched.

During one of the lulls in conversation, Judith leaned over to speak to Warren's daughter, "Oh, Natalie. I was just wondering if you could tell me who this person is? I saw them in some of your other wedding photos, too." Judith pulled out the card and pointed to the figure standing in the background behind herself and Warren. Natalie took the photo and frowned. She peered closely then shook her head, "No. I don't know him. He must be from Ben's side of the family."

Natalie tapped her husband on the shoulder, "Love, who is this guy?"

Ben looked, then rolled his eyes, "Oh, *him*! He was hanging around outside and when I asked who he was he said he was Uncle Jeremy. No... Jordan?"

"Joseph," Judith whispered. Ben snapped his fingers, "That's it! Uncle Joseph. So I assumed he was one of your mob and invited him in."

Natalie bristled, "What? No! He's not one of ours. Did you really just invite some dero in off the streets? To our wedding!?"

Judith paid little attention to the ensuing spat. For the rest of the evening and all the way through the drive home she barely spoke at all. At home she placed the thank-you card back among the Christmas cards and just stood there staring at it, her eyes unfocused.

"You forgot to bring in the mail." came Warren's voice from behind her, and she turned to see him drop a small stack of envelopes on the kitchen table. Judith staggered toward the table – her face white; her eyes expressionless. She shuffled through the envelopes until she found what she was looking for – a plain envelope marked "card only".

This one was handwritten, though, and in a familiar hand at that. Flicking it over Judith confirmed from the return address that this was, indeed, from her sister. "Another card?" asked Warren.

Judith glanced up at the display of cards on her cabinet before looking again at the envelope in her hands and finally responding, "No." She tossed the card, unopened, into the recycling. Perhaps nine cards was enough, after all.

Judith spent the rest of the evening tidying, rearranging things and generally just puttering around the house. "What are you *doing*?" Warren asked as she passed between the television and his armchair for the dozenth time.

"Just... getting things ready" Judith replied.

"For what?"

Judith didn't respond. Instead, she went to the guest room and made up the bed with fresh, red sheets.

TWELVE NIGHTS

KATHERINE KITCHENER

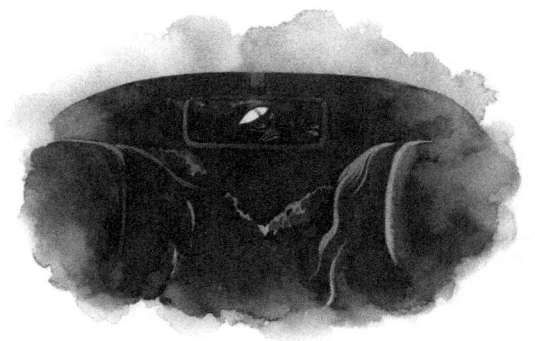

ROAD TOLL

"EIGHT." *MICHELLE'S* *VOICE* *CHIMED* mechanically. It was the first time either of them had spoken a word in over half an hour, but all Jared seemed to be able to do in reply was grunt. Michelle gripped the handle on the inside of the passenger car door so tightly that her knuckles were white.

This wasn't the first time they had visited Jared's parents together, but it would be the first time they were there together for Christmas and Michelle, a nervous passenger at the best of times, was particularly anxious about the holiday traffic. In the weeks leading up to their trip she was prone to rattling off statistics on the Christmas holiday road tolls. Apparently, there had been thirty reported deaths on the road nationally last year in the few days leading up to Christmas. Seven of those were in Victoria. It was actually less than in each of the last five years, but that fact didn't seem to set Michelle's mind at ease. She talked about how people were always rushed around this time of year trying to arrive at their holiday destinations before Christmas, how they didn't pay attention to the speed limits and didn't take enough breaks to avoid getting drowsy. At every Christmas party they went to she would comment on the fact that there were *so many* parties at this time of year and people drank *so much* and then just got back in their cars. There were more cops on the roads, but they couldn't catch *everyone*.

To keep Michelle happy Jared had agreed to take what he called the "John Denver" route home to his parents' place. They would eschew the freeways and main roads and stick to the smaller roads that meandered from one country town to the next. They both thought they might even see some interesting sights as they made their way across country Victoria, but mostly what they saw was a whole lot of nothing. Most of the towns were like facsimiles of each other. There would be the pub (or, more often, pubs) the post office, the supermarket – Usually either a Foodworks or IGA. If you passed a Coles or a Woolies you felt for a moment like you had rejoined civilisation. Almost.

As for the scenery, there were paddocks upon endless paddocks of dried grass. Jared tried to tell himself that this was just part of his homeland's natural beauty – *green and golden and green again* – but he knew this was not entirely true. The Reality was that climate change meant that what was once a cycle had become, essentially, permanent. It couldn't even truthfully be called a drought. Droughts broke. *We'll all be rooned*, Jared thought morosely. At least there were some signs of wildlife. Kind of.

"Nine," came Michelle's voice from the passenger side, as if on cue. Jared took a deep breath and decided to try again. "What was that one?" he asked with forced pleasantness. "Roo," Michelle responded. "Big one." This didn't give Jared much to work with so they sank once more into silence. Only it wasn't silence really, either, because Michelle insisted on playing Christmas carols on the car radio. The insistent, insipid jollity grated on Jared's nerves, but Michelle maintained it didn't feel like Christmas without them. She had, of course, never worked in retail.

"Pull over," Michelle demanded curtly and Jared obliged. "Are you gonna chuck?" he asked with genuine concern, but Michelle was already out of the car, slamming the door behind her.

Although he was not the anxious one of the couple, Jared felt uneasy with Michelle wandering out into the night in the middle of nowhere. He felt somewhat conflicted, though, as Michelle liked her privacy and had only recently accused him of 'hovering'. By way of compromise, he opted for watching her through the rear-view mirror, deciding that this gave one degree of separation, at least.

As Jared watched, Michelle tracked back a few metres to a small bit of scrub beside the road, where she crouched down. *So she's going to be sick, after all* Jared thought, his own stomach tightening in sympathy. She wasn't there for long, though, before she straightened up and strode purposefully back towards the car.

Jared looked back at his hands, still at ten and two on the steering wheel, and waited for the passenger door to open. He was surprised to instead hear the sound of the boot creak open, only to be slammed shut again a few moments later. Looking back in the mirror, Jared saw Michelle heading back to her spot by the road, the old woollen picnic blanket slung over her left arm.

Confused, Jared followed his girlfriend out. By the time he reached her she was once again crouching by the side of the road. She wasn't being ill, but he felt all at once that *he* may be.

In the light cast by his car's tail lights, Jared saw a thick smear of blood running from the centre of the road to a large, humped form in the bushes, right beside where Michelle was bent over. It was another dead roo, or so Jared assumed from the size. Honestly whatever the poor thing was in life it was now mangled beyond recognition.

"It must have been a truck," Jared breathed. His eyes were drawn to the creature's head, twisted at an unnatural angle from the body. The thing's face was torn all the way from mouth to ear, exposing what seemed like far too many teeth in a rictus grin. The only visible eye was rolled back far in the gaping socket, revealing an expanse of bloodshot sclera. The effect was somewhere between rapture and hysteria and Jared had the uncomfortable feeling that the creature – irrevocably, unequivocally dead – was laughing at something just behind him.

Why was Michelle looking at this, Jared wondered. It was morbid, even for her. He turned to speak to Michelle, to call her back to the car, but as he turned he saw she was scooping something up in the picnic blanket. Something pink and translucent. And squirming.

Jared blanched as he realised what it was. He gathered himself and tried to steady his voice as he said to Michelle, "Do you want me to just... you know?"

Michelle glanced up and blinked several times without comprehension, until Jared's point finally penetrated and her eyes flashed in the moonlight, "No, I don't want you to *kill* it! *Jesus!*" She stood up, clasping the bundle close to her chest. "With all the farms we've passed there has to be a vet around here somewhere. We just have to keep it alive until the morning and take it to someone then."

Jared thought that with tomorrow being Christmas eve they would be unlikely to find a vet open, but he was too tired to press the point. How long could a joey survive outside its mother's pouch, anyway? Surely not the whole night. Not when it had already been at the side of the road for god-knows how long, possibly injured itself and, judging from what he saw of its size and colour, so very young.

Best just to wait for nature to take its course and then pick up the pieces of a traumatised Michelle in the wake of it all. *Just an average Saturday* Jared thought ruefully, then hated himself for thinking it.

As they returned to the car, Michelle climbed into the backseat with the joey. Jared started up the engine and 'Silent Night' started playing through the radio. He looked in the rear-view mirror and felt a sudden, sharp pang as he saw Michelle nursing the tiny creature. Suddenly an all-too-familiar anger welled up inside of him as he wondered, not for the first time, when it would be his turn to mourn.

From the backseat, the joey was making plaintive little whines and snorts, keening for its mother. The sound set Jared's teeth on edge. Michelle started crooning to the thing in her arms. *Silent night* Jared thought bitterly. *Half the bloody luck.*

Jared fixed his attention on the road ahead, or tried to, anyway. He couldn't get the image of the mutilated kangaroo doe out of his head. He saw the poor creature's unnatural smile, the cloudy eyes fixed on nothing, but somehow, impossibly, seeming to still *see*. Jared felt a jolt as he thought this.

He licked his lips "...Shelly?" he asked tentatively. Michelle did not stop her soft singing. Jared coughed and turned off the radio, then spoke a little louder, if no more confidently, "Shelly, hon? How did you know the joey was there?"

Jared waited for Michelle's response, but none came. Michelle stopped singing, then, and in the ensuing hush Jared found himself at once both wishing for the carols to resume and being too afraid to reach over to turn the radio back on. Eventually, he managed to surreptitiously dart his hand out and flick the radio back on, only to find they had lost the signal. Outside, the car's high-beams illuminated nothing but the seemingly endless line of tar ahead of them and the equally boundless expanse of dried-up scrub to either side of them. As for what lay behind them, it may as well have been nothing.

Perhaps she's fallen asleep, Jared thought to himself. Between the lateness of the hour, the soothing drone of carols and the monotony of the road it did not seem unreasonable that Michelle could have nodded off. Glancing in the rear-view mirror Jared could see Michelle's head lolling back into the headrest, though her grip on the blankets and their squirming inhabitant still seemed firm. Claw-like, even. Jared was vaguely aware of the radio picking up an unfamiliar song out of the static.

> *O come with me where hills are brown,*
> *And Christmas Bush grows wild...*

Jared gripped the steering wheel, his knuckles whitening. "Shelly?" he tried again, gently, and this time his girlfriend's head rolled forward and she met his gaze briefly before her eyes rolled back as though to look at something above or even behind herself. She started to laugh. It was a thin, delirious laugh, her lips stretched unnaturally, impossibly wide. The thing on her lap had become suddenly still.

> *...So we can make a Christmas crown*
> *To grace a Kingly Child.*

Despite the lateness of the hour, the tortuous nature of the road ahead and the ever-encroaching presence of trees and the occasional power poll, Jared was paying no attention to the road. Even as the car drifted off the road, Jared was unable to tear his gaze away from the rear-view mirror as he watched the person he loved more than anyone else in the world and realised that he did not recognise her at all.

KATHERINE KITCHENER

LILIES FOR THE ALTAR

FLOWERS DIDN'T GROW WELL in Yearrnjenong. It had always been a dull, grey place. True, there was always plenty of rain, but it was more like a kind of persistent mist and, although it could soak through your clothes and right to your bones in just a few minutes, it was somehow never enough to penetrate the soil. The sun, when it did shine, did so with such intensity that saplings shrivelled and young buds wilted before they could even bloom.

Jenny's garden was one exception. Surrounding her house on all sides was a riot of colour and fragrance. A kaleidoscopic array of different species all jumbled together. African violets alongside birds of paradise. Camellias bordered by tufts of perfumed stock. There were natives, too. Velvety kangaroo paws and spidery grevillea. The trees around her property were always full of birds and the air was full of beautiful, blue-banded bees. Her cat, a bright, white Persian named Lucy, would sit on the verandah railing in the sun (when there *was* sun) and lazily bat at the occasional bee. Lucy was Jenny's dearest friend and closest companion, as well as the sole reason she couldn't grow lilies in her garden. All varieties of lilies, and every part of the plant, are deadly poisonous to cats.

The garden had originally begun as a way for Jenny to occupy herself while recovering from the incident, which she really didn't think about anymore (or so she would insist to herself on those long nights when sleep wouldn't come). Since then, though, it had become an all-consuming passion. A vocation, almost.

Jenny's perfect garden was matched, after all, only by her pure faith. Together these were the reasons that Jenny always supplied the floral displays for her local church. Every week, Jenny would make the half-hour drive to town with her backseat full of bouquets and posies to fill the various vases that adorned St Therese's Catholic Church. To Jenny, arranging flowers was a kind of prayer – the ultimate appreciation of God's most precious gift. Also, though she had never admitted it to herself, her status as the sole provider of flowers to the church bestowed on her a status, and filled her with a pride, that was probably not entirely Christian.

On the third Sunday of Advent, Jenny was milling about after mass catching up on the local news (she would never have dreamed of calling it "gossip") and generally accepting compliments on that week's flowers, when Father Hingle approached her. "Father!" gushed Jenny, "Your homily today was beautiful! I simply can't wait to hear you speak on Christmas Eve."

"You're too kind," Fr. Hingle said humbly, "But,

actually Christmas Eve mass was exactly what I wanted to talk to you about."

Jenny's eyes brightened and she leaned in so close Fr. Hingle found himself having to take a step back. "I've just been thinking... Your flowers are always so lovely... but I was thinking it would be nice... 'festive', you know... if we could have some Christmas lilies for next week."

Jenny's smile faltered, but she quickly recovered and tried her best to deflect, "Well, yes, of course it should be festive! We'll have some poinsettia, Christmas bush, mistletoe–"

"–and Christmas lilies." finished Fr. Hingle

"... And Christmas lilies" Jenny agreed glumly.

Jenny tried all over town to find Christmas lilies but it seemed that everywhere was sold out. She knew they were popular, but she hadn't expected to be unable to find them *anywhere*. Jenny even drove to the next town, but the closest thing she could find was a droopy bunch of pink blooms at the local Woolworths. For some time she stood there grimly considering the lacklustre lilies, but ultimately she could not bring herself to buy them.

While Jenny had made the rounds looking for Christmas lilies, there was one thing – a person, specifically – she kept hearing about. There were rumours in the local gardening club. Things whispered beside the ferns in the garden department at Bunnings. Mutterings from behind the counter at the florist. People spoke the name with a mixture of reverence and animosity – Chris Thorne. Jenny had heard these rumours before. The unfortunately named Thorne grew, not roses, but orchids. Rare ones, too. Jenny had been past his house a number of times but from the sparse front yard there was no visible indication of the supposed treasures that lay behind. If the rumours were true, Chris Thorne's garden may even have rivalled Jenny's own, though she had always thought there was something oddly selfish, perverse even, about keeping such treasures so private.

According to some of the stories, Jenny remembered as she drove home from the Woolworths, Chris grew other flowers, too, though no one could say what kind. Could he have some Christmas lilies stashed away somewhere, hidden from the world?

Jenny considered this possibility. It was unlikely. Extremely unlikely. And, yet, what other options did she have left?

Once she got home, Jenny went immediately to the kitchen where, under the watchful gaze of Lucy, she bustled about messing mixing bowls and pots and pans at a furious rate, determined to whip up her signature date and walnut chocolate slice in record time. Once done, she swept out into the garden, deftly snipping off the best blooms of her favourite natives and gathering them together as an attractive spray all tied up with a blue silk ribbon.

Chris Thorne's house was a former housing commission unit, which had been sold off several decades ago. From the front, it still had that austere appearance all public houses had, almost as if no one lived there at all, and as she approached the front door Jenny wondered whether it was even possible for Thorne to have the kind of beautiful garden that people spoke of. She knocked, and in the silence that followed she felt the almost uncontrollable urge to turn around and run. What was she doing here, approaching a stranger to ask to plunder their garden of flowers they may not even have? It was all so ridiculous. She had almost decided to leave when there was a sudden click and the front door opened slightly.

Two rheumy eyes peered out from the gap in the door. "Yes?" came a cautious voice. Thorne was older than Jenny had expected, a decade or so her senior, and for some reason she felt relieved at this. "Good afternoon, Mr Thorne." Jenny began brightly, "My name is Jennifer Buckley. I'm so sorry to drop in on you out of the blue like this, but I've heard about your beautiful garden and, well, I was just wondering if you would be willing to give me a tour? I'm a bit of a gardener myself."

Thorne sniffed, but otherwise made no response, so Jenny continued "I've brought you some of my own flowers... and a chocolate slice."

At the mention of chocolate slice Thorne's dull eyes suddenly brightened and he opened the door. There was nothing remarkable about Thorne's appearance. A white, middle-aged man he was, perhaps, a little thinner than most and a little more stooped. He had a full head of hair, mostly grey, and wore a dark pair of jeans and a blue flannel shirt. He was so ordinary looking that Jenny had a hard time locking on to any of his features. It was like staring at a bowl of porridge.

Thorne reached out and snatched the plate of slice out of Jenny's hands then retreated back into his house vaguely muttering by way of invite, "Come on, then."

Jenny stepped through the threshold and looked about. The interior of Thorne's house was dim and almost as bare as the front yard. "Um, the flowers?" asked Jenny uncertainly, holding up her bouquet. Thorne snorted. "Just put them over there," he snapped, waving dismissively at an empty sideboard. *Thorne by name; thorny by nature,* Jenny thought as she gently lay down the flowers.

Jenny followed Thorne through to his kitchen, where he laid out the plate of slice almost reverently on the bench. Then, he turned around, and it felt to Jenny like the first time he had properly acknowledged her. "Now!" he said, rubbing his hands together, "You wanted to see my garden?"

Nothing about the front and interior of Thorne's house could have prepared Jenny for what lay out back. There were multiple hothouses and garden beds, all set up to imitate different climates. A whole biosphere somehow squeezed into a backyard that was smaller than average.

Thorne took Jenny on a tour of each of the different sectors of his garden, becoming more and more animated as we went along. Jenny did not know much about orchids, this was not really the climate for them, but Thorne's collection was frankly astonishing. Even aside from his obvious enthusiasm when giving the tour, the very fact that he had managed to grow so many beautiful orchids in an environment not at all hospitable to them was clearly a testament to his passion. Jenny felt a rush of affection for the strange old man.

In a greenhouse that stored some of Thorne's rarest orchids Jenny noticed, right in the centre, a large, bowl-like flower with an open lid. "Oh, goodness!" Jenny cried, interrupting Thorne in the middle of showing off one of his finest orchids, "Is that a pitcher plant? It's so big."

Thorne's face darkened. "*That,*" he said in steely tones, "Is just to keep the insects and other vermin away from the orchids. I wouldn't dream of using pesticides on my treasures."

"So..." Jenny began cautiously, "You do grow some flowers other than orchids?"

Thorne sniffed again, "Of course I grow other flowers! I'm a horticulturist. Not much of a garden with only one family of flowers, is it?"

"I... suppose not," Jenny returned weakly, once more uncertain of where she stood with this man. "Here are the ferns," Thorne declared, pointing to a tiny patch of garden near Jenny's feet, "... And here are the philodendrons. And over there, in that smaller hothouse, is where I grow my lilies."

Jenny's heart leapt as they approached the glass structure. Thorne lead her inside and Jenny gasped at the sheer array of lily varieties the old man had managed to squeeze into this space. Jenny recognised several varieties of arum lilies, tiger lilies and, in a large cluster by the far wall...

"Christmas lilies!" Jenny breathed, and with her next breath took in the scent that immediately sent her hurtling back to her childhood. "My mother grew these. The house would be full of these at Christmas time." Jenny sighed and closed her eyes. It was almost like her mother was standing right there. She could have sworn that if she'd reached out her hand she could have brushed her mother's skirt. She thought of her mother singing carols in a voice that was at once both lyrical and mechanical – like a music box. Jenny felt that if she listened very carefully, there among the lilies, she would hear that voice again..

... Thorne sniffed loudly. Jenny started.

"*Lilium Regale,*" the man pronounced deliberately. "A rather common species, but nonetheless lovely in its own way. Native to the western part of Sichuan Province in southwestern China..." Thorne droned on and Jenny zoned out, preferring to focus on the beauty and fragrance of the flowers and the bittersweet memories they evoked.

After some time, Jenny realised that Thorne had stopped talking and was regarding her intently. She panicked. Had he asked her a question?

"Um... I was actually wondering if you would be willing to sell me some lilies?"

"The bulbs?" Thorne asked warily.

"Oh, no!" Jenny replied hastily, "Just some of the flowers. They're for an arrangement at the church."

"Hmm," Thorne tapped at his stubbly chin, "How many are we talking?"

"Just eleven of the Christmas lilies if you would be so kind."

"Not an even dozen?"

"No," Jenny said with confidence, "Odd numbers just... look better."

Thorne nodded. "You can have eleven. Do you want them delivered to your place or the church?"

Jenny felt strangely uneasy about giving Thorne her address and so she replied. "To the church, please. St Therese's on Puckle street. If you could have them delivered by 10 pm on Sunday, ahead of midnight mass, that would be perfect."

"Done," Thorne replied. Jenny could not believe it had been this easy. She could not believe that Thorne would so readily part with his flowers... but perhaps it would have been a different story if she had asked for orchids.

"How much do I owe you?" she asked.

"For a fellow apostle?" Thorne said with an oddly crooked smile, "You can have them gratis." Jenny found herself stunned again. She had not realised Thorne was religious. None of the rumours mentioned it, and she had certainly never seen him at Church. It was something else that should have raised the man in her esteem, but there was something off-putting about that crooked smile that made her edge her way out of the greenhouse and into the open portion of the garden. "You're too kind!" she gushed, all the while shuffling further and further away from him.

As she found herself once more among the orchids she cast her eyes about, trying to recognise the path back to the house. Even outside of the greenhouses, the garden was like a jungle (a strangely ordered jungle, of course) and she barely knew where to set her feet for fear of treading on some rare bloom. "And thank you so much for showing me your orchids. They're lovely. There's something about them that's oddly..." she cast about for the right word, "... masculine?"

Again came that crooked smile, "Well, you do know why they're called orchids, don't you?"

Jenny did, but she could not quite believe that this old man was really addressing her in this way, "I'm sorry?" she said nervously. Thorne leered at her, and without words reached down with one hand to adjust his pants.

Quick as a flash, Jenny spun on her heels and scurried down the nearest path, which luckily lead to a gate that took her out the driveway at the front of Thorne's house. "Thank you for your time!" she called behind herself, "I really must be off!"

*

On Christmas Eve, Jenny spent the day preparing the flowers for mass. She had decided on six identical arrangements of poinsettia and Christmas bush flanking the entrance and either side of the pews leading up to the altar. At the front of the altar itself would be the lily arrangement that Thorne would deliver later that evening. Assuming, of course that Thorne could be relied upon. "Of course he can," Jenny admonished herself firmly, "He said he was a Christian, after all." Jenny thought again of the man's lascivious expression and crude gesture, but quickly pushed the image out of her mind.

Jenny had positioned all her bouquets in what she had determined to be the optimum positions and she was rather pleased with the impact they made as one walked into the Church. All that was needed now was Thorne's lilies. Jenny wished she hadn't asked for them to be delivered so late. She wanted the flowers to be at their freshest, especially seeing they would be front and centre during the service, but she hated that she couldn't just finish things up herself now. She looked at her watch. 8 pm. Another two hours before she had planned for Thorne to deliver the lilies. She was worn out, having made multiple trips between her house and the Church throughout the day and decided that there was enough time to nip home once more and have a quick nap.

As she slept, Jenny had uneasy dreams. She was trapped in a jungle, or possibly a garden, and unidentifiable vines were twisting up and around her. Insistent tendrils were prodding at her, creeping into her mouth, up her skirts, beneath her eyelids.

Jenny woke with a start as her phone rang. She looked at the time. 11pm. Barely enough time to ready herself for midnight mass! Still groggy with sleep, she shuffled into her hallway and picked up the receiver. "Jenny, speaking," she croaked.

"Hello, Jenny. It's Fr. Hingle," came the familiar

voice. "I was a little surprised to not see you at the church yet, so I thought I'd give you a quick call."

"Oh, thank you, Father!" Jenny replied, flushing. I was actually just having a nap. I've been getting the flowers ready all day."

"Oh, yes. The flowers..." Fr. Hingle's voice trailed off.

"Is there something wrong?" Jenny asked uneasily.

"Oh, no! Nothing at all! The flowers are lovely as usual. It's just that... Isn't the centrepiece rather sombre for Christmas mass?"

"Sombre?" Jenny asked, still blinking sleep away.

"Oh, it's fine. Just not what I expected. I'm just glad to hear you're well and will still be making it to mass."

Jenny hung up. Confused, but more awake now, at least. She quickly slid on her best dress, deftly applied her makeup and then hurried out to the car, eager to reach the church in time to get a seat for the service.

Jenny did manage to get a seat, and right at the front (why did churchgoers always insist on filling up the pews from the back first?). She had barely looked at her floral displays as she entered the church. Just enough to assure herself there was nothing sombre about them. She thought them rather cheery, in fact. As she finally settled into her seat, however, she finally understood what Fr. Hingle was talking about. Out the front of the altar was the display that Thorne had evidently provided earlier that evening. He had provided eleven lilies. Eleven *perfect* lilies, in fact. They were not, however, the Christmas lilies that Jenny had requested but, rather, dead white arum lilies.

"It's like a funeral!" Jenny thought to herself with dismay. Not only that, but in addition to the lilies

Thorne had evidently decided to provide them with some of his precious orchids. Some sort of sanguine variety that drooped like flaps of raw flesh. Jenny was mortified. Throughout the entire service she could not stop staring at the obscene display. So fixated was she on this floral monstrosity that she didn't even hear Fr. Hingle's homily. Only the odd word or phrase broke through her daze. Virgin. Immaculate. Sacred body and blood. All the while, Jenny could not keep her eyes off the orchid's dewy folds. After a while, it began to seem to her like the entire display, lilies included, was twitching and pulsating. The flowers seemed to gape open like hungry maws. Opulent. Sensuous. Ravenous.

After the service, there was not the same level of cheer and festivity that one would normally expect on Christmas eve. Most people slipped away without a word and the few that hung back muttered and whispered to each other. They were talking, of course, of Fr. Hingle's strange homily, but Jenny imagined they were talking about the flowers. How could anyone fail to be offended by that arrangement? On the verge of tears, Jenny scurried off home without even waiting to speak to Fr. Hingle.

*

Jenny woke up late on Christmas day still feeling the lingering threads of last night's shame and disgust. She dragged herself out of bed and tried to put the whole incident out of her mind as she brewed her morning cup of tea. With no family of her own, Jenny had nowhere to go and no one to visit for Christmas and so planned to spend a quiet day with Lucy, pottering in the garden. After forcing down her tea and a single slice of sourdough toast, she dragged on her daggy gardening duds and headed out the front door.

TWELVE NIGHTS

What she saw when she stood out in her front yard and gazed at her beloved garden hit her like a blow to the gut. This was her garden, the same one she had spent over a decade growing and nurturing, and yet as looked at it now she no longer saw the beautiful symbol of God's creation. These were the same flowers that had been there yesterday, but rather than a tribute to the fertility of nature all Jenny could see was a fecund mass bursting with fleshy tumours. Every stamen protruding from voluptuous blooms was unrelenting in its singular purpose. Petals were decadently splayed to reveal the immodest pistils within the meaty hearts of the flower. Every tepal and whorl was like a nub of flesh, raw and exposed. The fragrance she once found delicate and sweet so now seemed rancid and noisome, like stale sweat and piss.

So repugnant was the sight that Jenny began to heave, though her stomach had insufficient content to actually bring anything up. How could this be? How could she have devoted her life to something she thought was so pure that had only turned out to be so... pornographic.

Jenny sobbed, but no tears came. She felt completely dried out and hollow inside, but she knew what she had to do. She went to her garden shed and grabbed her good shovel then immediately set to work digging up her once beloved garden.

It was a big garden, but Jenny worked tirelessly, without food or rest, and by the end of Christmas day where once had stood her garden was now just freshly tilled dirt and several heaping piles of upturned plants, their roots reaching desperately to the darkening sky.

I should salt the earth, Jenny thought to herself. *What could be purer than salt?* There were more pressing tasks at hand, however. Jenny went into her kitchen and grabbed the fresh packet of matchboxes that sat beside her gas stove.

*

It was early on Boxing Day when the fire brigade was called out to Jenny's property. Although there was a significant distance between Jenny and her nearest neighbour, the smoke was obvious, particularly given the total fire ban the region was under. The fire had obviously been burning for some time and although it, thankfully, hadn't reached the nearby bushland, the fire had encircled Jenny's house, obliterating her garden and scorching all four walls.

Jenny was found in her living room. At first, upon finding the body, firefighters assumed she had died of smoke inhalation. As the smoke gradually began to clear, however, they were shocked by how peaceful the woman looked – laid out like a saint with a beatific expression on her face. A black (once white) cat lay curled at her feet and the pair were wreathed by eleven slightly chewed, but perfectly white, Christmas lilies.

TWELVE NIGHTS

KATHERINE KITCHENER

TWELVE NIGHTS

NIGHT DIVINE

SHARON HUMMED SILENT NIGHT *SOFTLY* as she did *the* dishes, not because she was feeling particularly festive, although Christmas was only a few weeks away, but because she found the tune soothing.

All mothers worry about their children. Sharon reminded herself of this as she stood in the kitchen anxiously knotting the teatowel about her fist. Mothers worried and the children were alright. That was how the world worked. And yet, "It isn't right, Lucas being all by himself like that." Sharon said. She cringed as she heard the whine in her own voice, but this didn't stop her, "What does he even do out there? He's always coming back with scratches and bruises and he never says anything."

Scott sighed, "He's just a kid. He's just climbing trees, running around, you know? Having fun."

Sharon turned to face her husband, the teatowel wrapped around her knuckles like a bandage, "He's *twelve*!" she hissed, keeping her voice low. "He should have friends!"

"He *has* friends!" Scott scoffed, "What about Ben with the wonky eye? And what's-his-name... the Clancy kid."

"*Classmates*," Sharon insisted, "Neighbours. Not proper *friends*. When was the last time he visited another kid, or had one over here?"

At this, Scott rolled his eyes, "Seriously, Sharon? And if he had kids over here and they were sat in his room playing computer games all day you'd be worried about *that*."

Sharon pursed her lips and turned back to the sink. The dishes were done, but the kitchen window oversaw the backyard and she could watch to see when her son would emerge from the scrubby bushland at the back of their property.

Scott moved to stand beside her, placing a hand on her arm and gently turning her back towards him, "Look, honey, I know you're worried, but it's okay. *Really*. He's a good kid. He does well at school and he never makes a fuss. So maybe he's a bit of a... late-bloomer. Socially. So what? He'll come good. In the meantime, he's getting lots of fresh air and exercise."

"I guess so..." Sharon acquiesced reluctantly. Scott wrapped his arms around her "It's okay to worry. You're a mum. It comes with the job. But, really, he's okay. Tomorrow's Monday and he'll be at school and you can focus on your work again without worrying about him running around out there."

Sharon sighed and melted into Scott's hug. He was right. Everything seemed better when Lucas was at school and she knew he was surrounded by his peers. It really was just the weekends that seemed to make her anxious. The rest of the time she felt like they were a normal family... and they probably *were*. All mothers worried, after all.

Not long after, Lucas came back home for dinner, and as the three sat around the dining table chatting Sharon allowed herself to feel something like contentment. She breathed deeply, humming the tune to Silent Night in her head until the soothing melody made her taut muscles gradually unwind.

Lucas was talking excitedly to his dad about the latest superhero movie and Sharon felt a rush of affection as she watched her son's bright eyes and animated gestures.

"Can we, Mum?" Lucas asked, and Sharon started, realising she hadn't really been paying attention to what had been said, "Sorry, sweetie, what was that?"

"The *movie*!" Lucas said with a groan, "Can we go see it in the Christmas holidays? It's only a couple of weeks away."

Sharon blinked.

*

Sharon need not have worried about Lucas being alone. He had a number of good friends. Twelve, in fact. He was not sure how he had first found them. They had been with him as long as he could remember. In his earliest attempts to learn about them, he had read about poets seeing trees full of angels, but this seemed unlikely to him. Angels were, in his experience, solitary creatures and only showed themselves one at a time, each in their own season.

When the sun shone too hot and the blooms in his mother's garden began to wilt, Lucas would steal the last fading lilies and take them out bush to further inspect. There, among the drooping petals, he saw January's angel – a flicker of light, barely as big as a pinhead, that danced and fluttered between pistil and stamen while somehow touching neither.

In February, Lucas would find his angel friend roosting in the very tops of trees, so that he would have to climb up, up to dizzying heights, his knees scraping and his hands full of splinters, but it was worth it just to see their brilliant plumage of impossible colours.

Other angels writhed deep within the earth. In March Lucas would dig with both hands, not frantically but diligently, relentlessly, dirt caking under his fingernails and staining his cuticles black, until he uncovered the tiny, naked homunculus that wriggled grub-like among the hair-thin roots – pulsing with life and leaving in its wake a shimmering trail.

Because Lucas' birthday was in April this had always been his favourite angel. It was bulky yet oddly angular and would thunder through the bushland on hard hooves that left the earth undisturbed, even though it should have trampled it flat and muddy, scarring the landscape. Lucas would follow the thing's gleaming horns, his bare feet cutting on the same rocks upon which the angel's hooves sparked.

While Lucas had always known the angels, he had never known what to call them. He was certain they had names, but when he asked they would only twirl or dart; shiver or toss their great heads. His parents monitored his internet use closely, which curtailed his research somewhat. Lucas had only recently decided to risk scouring the school library for helpful material, and so found his favourite book.

*

Filing out of choir practice. Ben and his friends stifled snickers and nudged each other surreptitiously until they had turned the corner into the corridor and were safely outside of Mr Mullaney's earshot. Suddenly Ben's voice picked up, singing in mock-high tones, "Oh *cum,* all ye faithful!" while gesturing crudely with his right hand. His fellows guffawed loudly as they all peeled off to go to their lockers.

Between the lockers and the entrance to the changing rooms, Ben spotted a small figure (smaller than him, anyway) hunched up against the wall, book clutched tight in grubby hands. He sneered as he read the cover, "You *would* read a dictionary."

Lucas blinked dazedly. It was a few moments before the other boy's words actually seemed to penetrate. "It's a dictionary... *of angels,*" he clarified.

He was aiming for a note of scorn, Ben knew this – could see the arching of the boy's eyebrow – but in doing so Lucas had grossly miscalculated, because couldn't Ben also see the tremor in Lucas' hand? The slight hitch in his voice?

Ben scoffed then placed his palms together and rolled his eyes upwards, fluttering his lashes, "Dear God, *pwease* send me a guardian angel!".

A passing student, it didn't really matter who, laughed at this and Lucas reddened, hunching down further and raising the offending book like a shield.

Satisfied, Ben turned and strutted down the hallway, humming cheerily as he went.

*

And so Lucas learned the names of all his friends. In May an angel, pink and transparent, would slip among the creek pebbles. They had always evaded Lucas before, darting off if he so much as stirred the water with his breath, but Lucas now had a way to pin them down. "Ambriel" he whispered to himself, holding the name in his heart – a treasure uncovered, but just for himself.

In June, when he went to the southernmost border of his family's property and climbed the fence, sniffing at the air, and detected the exotic, yet familiar by now to him, fragrance of myrrh, he would know that it meant Muriel was close. He would then, as always, follow the scent into the bush where it mingled with the rot of unrecognisable plant matter and the sharp, acrid stink of beetles.

July would now bring Zarachiel, the angel who was at once the furthest and the one Lucas had to travel least to see. He would simply lie on his back in the front yard and watch the angel form themself among streaks of white cloud against the clear winter sky.

Lucas felt that now he knew Hamaliel's name, he would no longer feel the faint dread at the sight of that solitary figure which stalked the neighbour's wheat fields in August. While the many-pointed, golden crown atop the angel's head served as a promise of the crops to come, their elongated arms, cruelly curved, always put Lucas in mind of the reaping.

*

After over two decades of teaching, Mr Mullaney had learnt how to spot when a student was just mouthing along rather than actually singing. Most of the time he let it slide. In some ways, it was preferable to the caterwauling of an ungifted singer, but he could not abide such blatant and literal lip service when the class were practising hymns. After all, Mullaney thought, in singing, we pray twice, and to feign piety, especially during Advent – the lead-up to the most joyous time of year – was tantamount to blasphemy.

"Lucas, a little louder, please," the teacher cautioned sternly while the rest of the class continued. "Sing from your diaphragm."

At this, the boy blushed, then proceeded to lift his voice which at first quavered violently, "H-ark! The herald an-gels si-ng" before setting into a dull drone, "Glory to the new born king."

Mullaney winced. He tried to remind himself that a tuneless hymn was a prayer, nonetheless.

"Remember, angels are the voice of God. The least we can do to honour those messengers is to sing as well as we can. With gusto! Open your mouths!"

TWELVE NIGHTS

A certain dull note underlying the harmony had cut out and Mullaney scoured the class before his eyes alighted, once more, on Lucas. He wasn't even moving his mouth anymore and, instead, was looking curiously at Mullaney. He could not quite read the boy's expression, which discomfited him. After all his years of teaching he felt he knew just about everything there was to know about adolescent boys, but occasionally something came along that didn't quite fit within the established schema and that always threw Mullaney. He thought about pulling the boy up again, but something in that curious expression seemed to forbid it.

"Weird kid," Mullaney thought, bitterly to himself. "Enunciate!" he declared to the class.

*

Angels don't have voices. Unless the shuffling of wings is a voice. Unless the smell of fresh bread or the taste of honey is a voice. Lucas *knew* this and any suggestion otherwise seemed ludicrous to him. Offensive, even.

Lucas thought of this September just gone, when he had snuck off to the local quarry (where he was *absolutely* forbidden) and met there an angel of unsurpassed beauty (Jophiel, he now knew). Was he expected to believe that something so perfect and wise would speak in the same words as his teachers? Or his classmates, even?

Could a stone speak?

Could something as changeable as Barbiel, that slick green angel that slithered from unknown origins in the very heart of spring, stoop to the mundanity of the spoken word? He thought of the way the angel settled, like an oil slick, on the horse troughs and flickered and danced in the light. What was the angel supposed to be saying? "Hello"? "How's the weather?"?

And what about November? How could Adnachiel, who showed Lucas in visions of blinding radiance the true nature of things, speak in the same languages in which people told such poisonous lies?

No. Angels didn't speak. Not with words, anyway.

*

Scott liked to think of himself as a liberal man. He was, he would tell people, a feminist. He voted Green. He did his share of the cooking and cleaning and, today, the Christmas shopping. There was still, however, something of the traditionalist about him, which is why he winced when "Last Christmas" came on the store radio, even though it must have been the millionth time he'd heard it this season and he should, he knew, be used to it.

And then there was the matter of Lucas. What was to be done about Lucas? He told his wife not to worry and that everything was fine, was normal, but fathers worry, too. The truth is Lucas *should* have more friends.

And, while Scott didn't expect Lucas to tell him *everything*, the boy had given no indication whatsoever that he had any interest in girls. "Or boys!" Scott prompted himself, internally, because there was nothing wrong with that, either.

Lucas seemed to be trapped in a perpetual childhood and Scott knew of no way to reach his son to drag him out. The boy had asked for books, again, this Christmas and while Scott was vocally proud of the modesty of his son's request, he secretly wished he had asked for something more... *normal.*

Scott was wandering across the floor of Target, reluctantly meandering his way to the book section, when 'O Holy Night' came over the store radio. He stopped in his tracks. That had always been Scott's father's favourite carol. He remembered his father's rich voice and surprising range. Not always an easy man to get along with, but a beautiful singer. Scott took in a deep breath and closed his eyes. He felt oddly transcendent, as though on the verge of an epiphany. He opened his eyes and cast about looking for something to latch on to, but his fellow shoppers seemed unaffected by the dramatic change in background music. What he did see, through his daze, was a display of video game consoles.

*

Lucas lay staring at his bedroom wall. He was lying on his side right at the very edge of the bed to make room for the angel that lay behind him. Never in his life had he turned to see December's angel, but he knew they were there, their long, pale limbs a perfect mirror of his own form, curled there on the bed. They were just inches behind him and Lucas knew that if he just reached behind himself he would feel them there – could grasp their hand; could tangle his fingers in their hair. He never did, of course. To do so would violate the purity of that angel's presence. Besides, it was enough to know that he *could*.

Even among the angels, this one was special. While the other angels were all vaguely abstract in form, Lucas knew, without ever having to look, that December's angel looked just like the kind of angels you saw in books. A man. Like any man, only beautiful. Long hair and huge, white, feathery wings that were folded up behind them like a shield. Soft but inviolate.

The angel breathed in perfect unison with Lucas, so that they could not be heard. Occasionally, Lucas would slow down his breathing or stop altogether to try and catch the angel out, but it always matched him. Lucas smiled and whispered softly, reverently, "Nadiel".

At this, he sensed the angel stiffen. All at once ,Lucas gasped. It was like all of the air had suddenly been sucked out of the room. In the gap between Lucas' first desperate gasp and the next, he felt the angel's breath tickle the back of his neck, their perfect lips brushing his ear. They whispered a soft melody to him.

Lucas threw the sheet aside and stumbled out of bed – his eyes wide; clawing at his throat as he was unable to breathe. He didn't dare look around. *Angels don't speak*, Lucas thought.

But they sing.

He fell to his knees and rolled his eyes heavenward as all about him, all at once, he heard the cacophonous choir of all the angels' voices.